£2.95

from THE WOMEN'S PRESS

698763

Second Wave would like to acknowledge the help and support of Susan Croft, Pauline Jacobs, Cathy Kilcoyne, Carole Spedding and The Albany Empire Theatre. We are grateful for the financial support of the London Borough of Lewisham, Greater London Arts Association, the A.ts Council of Great Britain, the Inner London Education Authority, Sir John Cass Foundation and Marks and Spencer.

EDITED BY
ANN CONSIDINE
& ROBYN SLOVO

DEAD PROUD

FROM
SECOND WAVE
YOUNG WOMEN PLAYWRIGHTS

LIVEWIRE

First published by The Women's Press Limited 1987

A member of the Namara Group
34 Great Sutton Street, London EC1V 0DX

British Library Cataloguing in Publication Data
Dead proud: from Second Wave young women playrights.
  1. English drama—20th century
  2. English drama—Women authors
  I. Considine, Ann   2. Slovo, Robyn
822'.914'0809287   PR1272

ISBN 0-7043-4908-6

Typeset by MC Typeset Limited, Chatham, Kent
Printed and bound by Hazel Watson & Viney Ltd,
Aylesbury Bucks

Contents

This book is dedicated to the
young women of Second Wave

Introduction

The stage allows you to be different. You can be smart, awkward and bad. You can choose what you want to show, control what you express and take risks with other people. You are *doing* rather than watching; you are *making* things happen all around you.

Shopping Spree, the first play in this collection, is about girls wanting things, thieving and proving themselves. They carry out a series of well-planned raids on the local high street and "smile back . . . big and broad." In *Foreshore* Melanie risks her reputation and goes to the beach with the kind of boy who gets sand kicked in his face and who doesn't have a clue about talking to girls. These are both comedies in which the girls have the upper hand.

Dynette in *Backstreet Mammy* chooses not to accept motherhood while in *Dead Proud* another young woman chooses to keep her child and leaves home to survive on her own. Lesley hopes that by keeping the child, she may also keep the father. Both are taking steps to become independent, but in different directions.

Independence brings change, excitement and a kind of loneliness. In *A Netful of Holes* eighteen-year-old Angela makes up her mind to tell her mother she is leaving home. When she does leave, she leaves her childhood behind but also understands her mother's sense of loss. *A Slice of Life* presents a young black woman telling her friends that she has decided to stay on at school, while knowing that separation from her friends means losing them. *Ishtar Descends* is about a different kind of loneliness – a young woman's search for her own identity – linking myth with the modern world.

Other people's expectations can prove hard to live up to, and are sometimes even harder to understand. In *No Place Like Home* Marcie's mother asks, 'Why all you cannot do me proud?' This is what she expects: 'You and Trevor getting married? . . . buy a house? . . . married wid nice clothes . . .?' But home can also be a refuge for dreams. A daughter imagines Dominica to be full of the warmth and richness of her father's stories – where life is *good* – but she knows that he can never really go back. For her, a young black woman born in Britain, home is a passed-on memory.

Dead Proud introduces the work of several new black women playwrights. Some use patois from the different islands of the West Indies. For example, in *When Last I Did See You* the writer celebrates the humour and wit of Jamaican language and with this comes the feel of the place, the qualities of the people, their style and pace of life. In contrast, the intense atmosphere and character of the West Coast of Ireland is created in *Fallen*, a play about a young country woman accused of murdering her child. In both these very different plays the authors make a clear connection between the place and the people.

This book is about young women's lives. About dealing with a world in which you have little power, where there are often no real choices, where you have to jostle to be heard. *Dead Proud* is a preview of work from a new generation of women artists. Their voices challenge the voice of experience: their writing as varied in style and character as they are. These plays have been written to be performed, and they come alive when seen and shared with an audience.

The plays and extracts in this collection were among

two hundred and fifty, mainly from first time writers, submitted to the Second Wave Festival of Young Women Playwrights at the Albany Empire Theatre in South London. The aim of this Festival, and of our ongoing work, is to celebrate and encourage new writing for the theatre from black and white working-class young women whose voices are often not heard. Four plays were selected by a panel of judges led by Glenda Jackson to be produced and put on stage as part of the Festival in 1986 and two of these, the comedies *Shopping Spree* and *Foreshore*, were performed to young audiences in the Studio Theatre.

These scenes from young women's lives have been written to be played, to be read in your room, in theatres, youth clubs, in schools or wherever you can put place and people together. Devised plays like *A Netful of Holes* and *Slice of Life* came from just such meetings: from talking with friends and from workshop improvisation.

There is a spirit of resilience and toughness in this new writing: *Dead Proud* celebrates this energy, and the spirit of young women.

Ann Considine
Co-ordinator, Second Wave
London, July 1987

Shopping Spree

by Marie Wilson

This play may be acted solely by the six main characters – The Girls – who can also take on the roles of store detective, shop people and parents. Alternatively there can be a full cast of up to fourteen characters.

CAST

Willy Mandy Willis (the gang leader)
Coll Andrea Colley
Slingers Paula Slingsby

Skin Vicky Colley (Andrea's sister)
Choc Jackie Willis (Mandy's sister)
Pip Donna Willis (Mandy's other sister)

A store detective
A market stall holder
Vera Turner Shop assistant

Mr Turner Of the newsagents
Mr Jackson Of the Mini Market

Mrs Slingsby Paula's mum
Mrs Willis Mandy's mum
Mr Willis Mandy's dad

*Shopping Spree is a story told by the three main characters –
Mandy, Paula and Andrea ('The Gang') – sometimes directly
to the audience, often they mime events. There are many props
mentioned throughout but this can be made easier for
production if they are mimed. Lighting can be used to indicate
each change of scene.*

*It is 1977. That's not so long ago. In those days the fashion
was not what it is now, but girls who lived on big housing
estates in large towns were pretty much the same. The things
that girls like doing, and the adventures they go on are still
very similar . . . This is the story of one such adventure.*

*A girl appears on stage, she seems to have been accused of
something and speaks as if she is excusing herself.*

Mandy *(addressing the audience)* I don't know how it
started, I can't remember. Was it Rimmel eye
shadow? A twist-up stick of greasy crease-proof eye
shadow in Toffee Shimmer or was it Aquamarine?
Or was it the two-pound box of Bournville selection?
Plain chocolates with assorted centres. Oh, I don't
know, but I do know the rest.
(she introduces herself)
There was me, Mandy Willis. Eleven years old.
Known to me friends as Wild Willy Willis or Willy
for short. I was a smart dresser in those days. I wore
my hair scraped back *(she scrapes it back exaggerating
the movement)* off my face in a pony tail with spotted
ribbon in blue and white, and I wore round gold
sleepers and a big silver band on my finger that was
engraved with a lion and had 'LEO' stamped wonkily
across it. That was my knuckle duster in case any big
kids came and we had to fight with 'em. I had a
bomber jacket made of blue plastic, with a white zip
about two inches wide. And 'high waisters' or
'Oxford bags'. These were trousers with wide flared
bottoms and deep waistbands with loads of buttons.

7

They were very trendy, though I don't know why, because it took ages to get them on and off because of all the buttons, and the flares always got stuck in the chain of me bike. (*pause*) Anyway, picture me, if you can, dressed like that. Down at Lowedges Park with me gang, me mates, friends, the girls. Andrea 'Coll' Colley and Paula 'Slingers' Slingsby.

Enter Andrea and Paula. They describe themselves to the audience

Andrea (Coll)   Andrea Patrisha, pronounced Pat-reeshah, Colley. Blonde hair blue eyes. Eleven years old. I've been friends with Mandy since I was five years old. We used to have pegs next to each other in infant school. Mine had a lovely swan picture on it and Mandy's was a ladder. My nickname is Coll or Colley.

Mandy (Willy)   You can imagine what she's wearing just from the sound of her voice! Purple T-shirt, with 'Paris' on it in fuzzy black letters stamped all over, accompanied by a wobbly outline of a winking lady's face. A dark purple corduroy skirt with lace on the bottom, white knee socks and white lace up plimsolls – sweet, well she looked it at least. Then there was Paula.

Paula (Slingers)   Paula Slingsby, the eldest. I am twelve. When I'm not helping my mum doing the ironing or washing for all our family, I meet Willy and Coll at the bottom of our road. They don't half make me laugh. Even when they laugh at me I just laugh anyway, they're so funny, and me mum says 'If you don't laugh you have to cry'. Sometimes though, I've scared them something wicked. Once, right, we were round at my house. It was the night when Mum went to Mecca Bingo. We were in the living room

8

talking about schools and boys and all the stuff you talk about in secret. Then I remembered a trick that my brother showed me. Right, look – sit like this with your backs together.

Andrea What you going to do Paula?

Mandy Yeah what's the big idea, ey?

Andrea If it's a 'why don't you' trick, forget it.

Paula Colley shut up.

Mandy Yeah Colley wobbles! Shut your mouth. Go on Paula, show us.

Paula OK
(*to the audience*) I moved over and turned the lights off . . . (*switches off light. Fade out*) And went back to them feeling my way past the leather-look settee, I can feel the hole in the back. Our David did that with his camping knife when he thought his gold ingot was down the back of the cushions. It wasn't all that was there. There was two felt tips, four one pences, a bottle top, a hair pin and the back of an earring. I move on, to the old wooden chester drawers. The heavy wood drawer creaks open – 'creak' – and I take out what I need. I sit with them. (*takes a hand torch from the drawer*) 'Ding'.

Torch on

Andrea Oh God, hurry up Paula, I've got to get home.

Mandy Shut up, it's good this.

Paula covers torch making a giant shadow of a hand

Andrea Oh my God!

9

Mandy Sssh!

Paula (*in a scary voice*) You are trapped inside this jar, there is no way you can escape. The only way out is into the hand of the Night Giant. He will lift you out and crunch you in his teeth, until your blood spurts and your bones snap!

Andrea Uuugh!! Stop it now, it makes me feel sick.

Mandy Oh no. Colley Wobbles look, the hand, it's coming.

Paula The Giant is unscrewing the jar . . . (*mimes action*) his hand dips inside, who will he choose . . .? A blonde with blue eyes like the sky, and yellow hair like butter.

Mandy It's you Colley.

Andrea Oh no, leave me, give up, leave me!

Paula Too late, the hand approaches. Nearer and nearer, nearer and nearer . . .

Andrea No!

Paula Yes! (*fast and unexpected*) It's got you Colley!! (*torch off*)

They roll about in the dark, squealing.

Paula (*to the audience*) Suddenly the lights go on. (*lights up*) And standing there is my mum . . . (*mimics mum*) 'Paula go to bed, now. I will talk to you later, you two you better run home. It's dark outside and you should have been in an hour ago, if I know your parents. And from now on I want *you* in on your own when I play Bingo. You, bed. (*to the others*) Home.' (*to audience*) I was quite lucky to just get sent to bed really, because my mum gets easily annoyed at any 'funny business'. It was worth it to see Colley

Wobbles, whiter than white, scared stiff. She's such a bighead, she thinks she's Mandy's only friend. I know she tries to make Mandy like her more than me, it won't work though. We're a gang, not like those other girls at our school who walk along arm in arm, like a bunch of sissies.

Andrea (*to audience*) Paula – or 'Slingers' as she is known – is wearing a green knitted dress, a fluffy blue cardigan and red knee socks with no elastic in them and black plimsolls. She wanted lace up ones like Mandy's but had to have elastic fronted ones because she's got broad feet.

Mandy (*to audience*) It's Saturday morning, a grey damp day, the sky is white and the trees are bare. The gang are sitting in the bus shelter at Termo Shops. We call them Termo Shops because it's short for terminus! Anyway, Termo Shops, or Lowedges Shops to give them their official title. (*pause*) It's small with a roundabout in the middle. There's not many shops and no station, but it's busy with people. Lowedges Shops. A butcher's, a baker's, but no candlestick maker's, instead a fruit shop. Boring. There's Fashion Clothes, whose existence seems to depend on aunties and mums buying acrylic jumpers for each other's birthdays, and supplying the girls of Lowedges Estate with enough knicker elastic to play french skipping until they reach a hundred. And when they reach a hundred or even sixty they can have their hair cut for seventy-five pence on Tuesdays at Scissors Hair Stylists because that's pensioners' day.

Paula (*to audience*) There's a kebab shop. It's always shut on a Saturday morning. The windows are covered in greasy finger prints and there's usually a big pile of sick just outside. Ugh!

Andrea (*to audience*) Sometimes we see the spew a bit further up the road and we always say it must be someone called Mr Iron Belly who managed to carry it that far before regurgitating! (*mimes vomiting*) For those of you who don't know what that means, you should listen in biology lessons instead of writing notes to your friends. Paula's brother calls it the Botulism Bar, because that means food poisoning.

Andrea (*to Paula*) Food poisoning! Did you get it Paula? . . .

Paula Yeah.

Andrea . . . I've told you not to eat them kebabs!

Paula Funny. (*to audience*) There's a betting shop as well. We're not old enough to go in there. My dad spent half his life in that shop, so me mum says. Mind you that can't have been long, because he died when I was four. My mum says he's better off, and so is she because now no one pinches her housekeeping money to back the horses.

Mandy (*to audience*) Then next door to the betting shop is the Post Office where our mums go to get the Family Allowance. We used to go and fetch it for Mum when she was working sometimes, and we'd say: 'Mum how come we can't have this money all to ourselves if it's for us' and she would say, 'If you can manage to buy yourselves everything that I buy you now with that money alone, then you're welcome to it'! But it always sounded as if we'd be worse off, so we never took it any further than that. And apart from the different coloured stamps on display, the Post Office was boring as well. But there was always the chemist. A magnificent glittering arcade of eyeshadow, mascara, lipstick, nail varnish. Perfume and talc sets. All colours and smells. Jasmine, Iris,

Fern, Lily of the Valley, Blue Hyacinth, Lavender and Musk, which was reported to make boys 'fancy you'. There was men's stuff in the chemist too. There was soap-on-a-rope in the shape of footballs for dads and brothers, and there was Brut aftershave for men. That was for your boyfriend, if you had one. None of us did, did we? . . .

Paula/Andrea Na!

Paula 'Cause we're the gang!

Andrea The girls!

Mandy The hardest, craftiest . . .

Paula Cleverist, funniest . . .

Andrea Ace-ist, in Lowedges and . . .

Mandy (*continues to audience*) We were telling you about the chemist. All this corn plasters and toilet rolls, highlighted by blinding fluorescent tube light. Now we're talking! And there's the paper shop that sells all manner of delights from chocolate mice to fountain pens, from *My Guy* to *Old Moore's Almanack*. From cheese and onion crisps to Wilsons' No. 1 Snuff. And dominating the grubby terrace of shops is Jackson's Mini Market, a fine emporium packed to the ceiling with bargains galore, windows ablaze with posters proclaiming, in felt tip pen, the latest and greatest price reduction ever.

(*to Andrea and Paula*) So, what's nicking rate on the chemist then?

Andrea It's supposed to be dead easy, innit Paula?

Paula Yeah.

Mandy Come on then, what are we waiting for?!

Andrea (*to audience*) And no sooner said than done

Paula . . . we're in the chemist . . .

Mandy . . . it's warm and quiet . . .

All . . . we're browsing . . .

They all adopt 'browsing' posture. Andrea mimics the shop assistant

Andrea 'Do you want anything love?'

Mandy No thanks, we're just looking.

Paula (*to audience*) I really *was* just looking. I was terrified, it's not that I'm not into it. Well it is, in a way. I have a dream about it. There's me and Mandy and Andrea, we've all got our pockets bulging with goodies. Real daft stuff like a bike and coats and a big box of chocolates. But it's real, in my dream it seems normal. We're walking through this big shop, like the Army and Navy. I'm at the back, Andrea turns round, she looks past me, horror on her face. Then her and Mandy are running, running like the wind to the lift, the doors are open. I try to run but it's one of those dreams where you just can't move, no matter how hard you try. They're shouting to me from inside the lift. (*Mandy and Andrea stand close behind Paula*)

Mandy/Andrea Paula! Paula, run! Store detective.

Paula (*to audience*) I'm still trying but they seem to be moving away, not getting closer. Then the doors shut and I hear a voice behind me (*as the store detective*) 'Paula Slingsby – I believe' (*as herself again*) Then I wake up with a jolt. Ahh! I'm in bed, the sheets are all over the floor, I'm sweating, it's horrible. I can't stop thinking about it when I'm in the chemist, so I don't pinch anything and I stay away from Mandy in case she gets caught.

Mandy (*moves towards audience*)   At this point I was *so* brave. I felt no fear. I had what me mum would have called 'bare-faced cheek'. I was brave, cool, brazen and quick!! Nicking stance. (*adopts position*) Facing assistant in shop. Browsing. Watch her eyes and when she goes under the counter. Snap . . . Grab . . . got 'em. There you go, you see my friends! The hand is quicker than the eye. No messin'. The assistant looks up and she smiles. Even better, she hasn't suspected a thing! And so what can I do, me, Wild Willy Willis, cunning master thief of Lowedges, but smile back like this, big and broad! (*grins*) She goes in the back to get a prescription form. One-Two-Three, like lightening – two kohl eyepencils and a lipgloss, gooey roll-on type – cherry flavour. Delicious. (*Andrea stands behind her, looking agitated*) I sense an irritating presence at my left elbow, and look round. It's Colley, red faced and shifty looking, scared stiff, a born coward. All gob and no action.

Andrea (*to Mandy*)   Come on Willy, let's go.

Mandy   No. I want one of them Mix 'n' Match shaders in burnt chocolate and coffee.

Andrea   Oh, get us one in turquoise.

Mandy   No chance, get it yourself.

Andrea   I daren't.

Mandy   Tough. Now shut up or she'll hear you . . . (*to audience*) And like a flash it's in the pocket and we're off. But before we go I buy a red glucose lolly, cost three pence. And the assistant says: 'Bye love'. (*pause*) Outside in a gennel* about a hundred yards sprint away, constantly looking back to make sure

---

*A South Yorkshire word for alley way.

we're not being followed, we look at the spoils. (*she joins the others*)

Andrea/Paula (*to Mandy*) Let's see, let's see, ah, brilliant! (*Mandy hands them the 'swag'*)

Mandy (*to audience*) We sit back on our heels in a huddle and feast our eyes. The two eye pencils are very pleasing. One in olive green and the other a purple colour called Grape Sorbet. Then there's the Mix 'n' Match Shaders, well, that's mine really but we're going to share it. And best of all the cherry lip gloss, sticky and thick, makes your lips look as if they've had a coat of varnish. We all put some on, me first (*she does*) then Colley (*carefully and flirtish*) then Paula (*clumsily and enthusiastically*) Beautiful!!! (*blows a puckered kiss*) We end up ruining most of our spoils, mainly because nobody wants to take them home, for if their mums see them . . . We get rid of the kohl pencils by defacing the bus shelter. We write:

Andrea (*mimes action*) 'Andrea Colley loves Mike Brothwell.'

Paula (*mimes*) 'Paula loves David Farrell.'

Mandy (*to audience*) And when it's my turn to write (*she does so*) . . . 'I woz ere, ere I woz, woz I ere 'cause I woz!' The nib runs out so we kick them all down a grate near the 75 bus stop. (*pause*) It was a regular thing. I was never scared, never worried about being caught, I thought I was invincible. I lay in bed at night looking at the shapes in the woodchip paper, and I thought there's as much chance of me getting caught as there's of Coyote catching Road Runner.

Andrea You wouldn't catch me nicking anything. Well you couldn't if I hadn't, could you? Anyway my reasons are simple, I think about the future. I mean, you couldn't get a job as a policewoman if you got caught pinching could you? My mum told me that there was a policeman once – did a raid on a house where there were supposed to be squatters, but there weren't.

Mandy Typical.

Andrea (*to audience*)   While he was in the house he saw a stamp album, had a quick peek at it because he was a keen collector himself, and saw a stamp that he really wanted. It was rare, and he'd wanted it for years. 'Course he couldn't help but steal it; and of course he couldn't help but show it off either. One day he showed it off down the station, which was unfortunate! . . . so PC Stampstealer lost his job. Now when I think of that I, personally, like to keep my hands clean. But if you're given something as a gift after it's been stolen, that's okay. As Mum says to me when our Eddie brings home the free meat from work: (*she mimics Mum's voice*) 'We got it as a present, it wasn't us that pinched it.' I agree with that. I don't mind taking stuff from Mandy after *she's* nicked it. I get some free stuff and if she gets caught I get away with it! It's the best way.

Mandy (*to audience*)   I couldn't understand why Andrea wouldn't pinch anything, but when we shared the spoils she wanted the swag. I didn't like it. I used to think, if she wants it why doesn't she get it herself? But she's smarter than that. Which I didn't like either. One day we were in Jackson's Mini Market and I had two bars of Galaxy chocolate, a Jif lemon, a packet of processed cheese and a carton of hundreds and thousands. Andrea walked in front of me with her Womble bag on her elbow. (*they play out the scene. Andrea stands as if holding a bag*) Suddenly on impulse I picked up a packet of Club biscuits, and skilfully lowered them into her bag. With a smart flick of the wrist, I slipped her address book over them. She walked on oblivious and we left the shop . . . (*they run out of the shop*) When we got to Lowedges Park, running and laughing all the way, we looked at the stuff. We sat in the wooden slatted box at the top of the slide and ate the cheese and chocolate. I squirted the lemon on kids who tried to get up the steps; (*she does so*) 'Get down'. Later on, round the back of the cricket pavilion, we squashed the hundreds and thousands into patterns in the soft mud and I said: 'What did you get Coll?'

Andrea (*to Mandy – amazed*) Nothing.

Mandy Are you sure, look in your bag then! (*to audience*) Realisation dawns on her pale face, she grabs the bag and looks in it. Nearly crying she splutters out:

Andrea (*holding the biscuits*) Oh my God, you 'orrible git! What did you do that for? I could have got caught.

Mandy Yeah, well, now you know what it's like don't you? (*to audience*) Ah! Silence follows. And then I say (*pause*) 'Are you walking home or what?' (*they move off. To audience*) And soon enough we're meandering home eating Club biscuits and laughing again . . . 'Things have got to get worse before they get better,' that's what my mum used to say. Well, for us it seemed the other way around. We started getting a bit more adventurous, our horizon suddenly broadened and we hit the High Street.

Paula Now we're talking *big* shops, like Marks & Sparks, Woolies, and the markets.

Andrea We had plenty of markets to choose from, each one holding infinite delight for a gang of light-fingered imps like us.

Mandy They were my favourites, they always had a good feeling of gypsyish excitement like the olden days. I loved that feeling; *pure* excitement, it tore through me like an electric shock. In there I felt like the Artful Dodger, Harry in my Pocket, even Houdini, a magician making things disappear from a stall, and appear later in my own pocket, before your very eyes! I was a con, a trickster, a knave, a conjurer of a unique kind. The Market . . . think of it as Petticoat Lane, it was very similar. (*enter stallholders and customers. Market stall voice*) 'And while I'm at it I'll throw in a description, not for five pounds, not for four pounds, forget that. Put your money away, because I'll tell you what I'm gonna do . . . you can have it *free* with the rest of this story!!' (*she moves around the market*)

A myriad of stalls selling all manner of goods, a shoplifter's paradise – that's what we called it. Earring stall first. Earrings! Long dangly ones, studs all shapes all sizes, plastic, gold, silver, hypo–allergic sleepers. Gold ones, silver ones, diamond cut, plain, any sort. Little round discs, with strange engraved lines on, that when you blew or spun round, words appeared like: 'He loves me' or 'Hi there'. (*pause*) 'Scuse me Missis.

Stallholder Yes love.

Mandy How much are these brass horse shoes, hung up there behind you? (*to audience*) She turns to look, and by the time she looks back the earrings are in the pocket!

Stallkeeper They're two pounds fifty love.

Mandy Oh, I might get me mum one for her birthday.

Stallkeeper You don't want one now then?

Mandy   No, I'll have to save up first . . . (*she moves on. To audience*) Next stop haberdashery and underwear. Matching bra and knicker sets in sealed plastic packets. Made in Taiwan, 100% cotton. I'll have the one with pink roses on. Andrea can have the one with dog faces because she's not nicking. It's, like, danger money, the more you risk the more you get. Aero bars, Rubettes scarves, Jackson Five mirrors, Womble pencil cases, fluffy purses with plastic faces and zip tops. And still I'm cunning fearless Al Capone Willis, that's me! . . . One day, the 'piece de resistance' competition. Cream eggs. How many . . . in one go?

Andrea (*to Mandy*)   Jane Winters got five. I bet you can't beat that.

Mandy   I bet I can. Can I? Yeah, 'course I can. Let's go.

They move away from the market and Mandy enters the shop. Mr Turner is watching carefully, stepping from foot to foot

Mandy (*to audience*)   Inside the paper shop there's Hawkeye Turner of Turner's News. He watches like a vulture. It's like those films on telly when someone's lost in the desert with no water and the vultures all gather, waiting for them to die. Me? I'm browsing, as ever. (*she does*) The shop's brimful of goodies, rich pickings – Silvine drawing pads, paper clips in assorted colours, drawing pins, balls of string, sellotape, reporters' notebooks, biros – red, black and blue. Pencils, crayons, rubbers – Ruffle bars, Mars bars, Twix, Frys chocolate cream and last but by no means least, Cream eggs. The phone rings (*Turner moves to back of shop*) . . . Turner's in the back answering it, and I'm there like Jumping Jack Flash (*grabs eggs and puts them in her pocket*) . . . One-Two-Three-four-Five (*grabbing handfuls*) Six-Seven-Eight. I've already got nine when he says:

Mr Turner Vera, come down here and mind the counter will you? I'm talking to our Walt on the phone.

Mrs Turner (*offstage*) Coming.

Mandy (*to audience*) But she's not fast enough for me, I think for a second and then I chance it. I grab as many as I can, until I hear her foot on the stair (*pause*) but she's too late. I've got them all safe in the hole in my pocket and down into the secret depths of my coat lining. (*enter Mrs Turner*) As she enters through the doorway behind the counter I'm poised cat-like, holding up a fizzy Cola bottle made of jelly (*holds it high*)

Mrs Turner Cola bottle? One pence please lovey.

Mandy Thanks . . . how much are Cream eggs?

Mrs Turner Nine pence lovey.

Mandy Oh!

Mrs Turner Never mind lovey, you might get one for Easter, eh?

Mandy Yeah . . . (*moving out of shop, to audience*) She smiles. So do I. Then I'm outside. Running like the wind. 'Dur dur dur dur dur!!!' (*singing tune from Six Million Dollar Man. To audience*) I don't wait for Andrea and Paula, and minutes later they come breathless from sprinting, and we lay laughing in the subway outside the 'Rice Bowl' chip shop.

Andrea/Paula Willy – what happened?

Mandy (*to audience*) I tell the story . . . (*to the others*)

'You might get one for Easter, if you're lucky.' Oh yeah, well I doubt it . . . 'cause I've got at least nine in my pocket at this very moment. (*they all laugh*)

Paula How many did she get, Winters?

Andrea Five.

Paula Yeah, beat that did you?

Mandy (*to audience*) Me, pretending to be modest. (*to Paula*) Well I did get a couple more. *Only* seventeen! (*to audience*) They howl in disbelief, but soon enough the eggs are lying nestled in our hands. Seventeen! Seeing is believing.

Andrea Bloody hell, Willy, some snatch!

Paula Yeah.

Mandy (*to audience*) However all things come to an end. A spanner appeared in those smoothly running and highly successful criminal works . . . (*enter Choc, Pip and Skin*)

Paula (*to audience*) Mandy's sisters, Choc and Pip, and Andrea's sister, Skin. In the school holidays they have to come with us because there's no one in at home. We have to watch what we say, because they can drop Mandy and Colley in it. We're talking, they're listening. The gang are leaning on the railings next to the garages. Andrea's telling the only joke she knows – again!

Andrea (*telling them the joke*) . . . so he comes to this other animal and he says (*fingers pulling mouth open*), shello, shi'm a wide moufed fwog and I eat shlugs and shnails. What are *you*? And the crocodile replied: 'I'm a crocodile and I *eat* wide-mouthed frogs! So the frog says (*purses her lips to tight O shape*) 'Oh, you don't see many of those about do you!

Choc/Pip/Skin Heard it. Ancient or what?! We want news not history!

Mandy (*moving in*) All right. Shut up then, you pests!

Choc You're not our mum you know.

Mandy I'll be Dad in a minute and then you'll wish I *was* Mum.

Skin Anyway you'll never guess what *we* did today when we went to Jackson's.

Andrea does cartwheels and handstands.

Andrea (*standing on her head*) What? What did you do?

Pip Guess! (*they laugh gleefully and introduce themselves to the audience*)

Choc The twins Jackie and Donna, nicknamed Choc and Pip.

Pip Pip, because I'm small!

Choc Choc, because I used to stuff myself all the time with sweets and chocolates.

Skin My real name is Vicky, but they call me Skin because I'm skinny. (*to audience*) We could keep them guessing about what we've done, but they'd be mad so we only hold back for a bit. After they've guessed about fifty things, like –

Choc Dropped a match down the maisonnette's rubbish shute . . .?

Pip/Skin No!

Pip Let off a stink bomb in the butchers . . .?

Skin/Choc No!

Skin Nicked a washing line to make a rope swing?

23

Choc/Pip No!

Skin You must be joking, it's better than that!

Mandy (*to the girls*) What is it then, borers? Tell us before we fall asleep!

Choc (*to Mandy*) We nicked some stuff today!

Mandy You what!! (*to audience*) My legs weaken and I have to sit down on the steps. I shout to Andrea who's walking on the garage roofs, dropping pebbles on the boys who are playing at 'Space 1999'. (*shouts*) Andrea – get down. I want you, it's serious. (*she joins others. Lights down to indicate that they are in the refuge shelter*) Fifteen minutes later we are in the brick-built room that houses the massive communal dustbin for the maisonnettes. It's dark and smelly but with the door shut it's secret. (*to Choc, Pip and Skin*) Listen, it's not just a laugh you know. It's serious. If you get caught you get done.

Andrea Yeah . . . think about your future.

Paula You could be in trouble, imagine your Mum and Dad. What would they think?

Pip (*cheekily*) *Are* we planning on getting caught though . . .!?

Mandy Look, you don't know, do you? I think you're too cocky by far. That's a sure sign you could get caught! (*to audience*) *Actually* she reminded me of myself. I saw them as my apprentices. Three trainee tea leafs. I had an idea, a test to see what they were made of. (*she pauses, talks to herself*) . . . Willy, you *fool*, what are you thinking of? Try to put them off. Scare them . . . (*to audience*) I come to a compromise and start to tell Paula and Andrea my idea. We have a gang discussion. We hatch a plot. If they want to steal we should let them. (*turns to Choc, Pip and Skin*) Right you lot, this is the plan. If you're foolish enough to steal, we'll make it hard for you, and maybe then you'll leave it alone.

Andrea (*joining in*) . . . RIGHT!?

Choc/Pip/Skin   Yeah. We're not scared. We know what to do, you know.

Mandy   Do you. (*to audience*) So we gave them a list of things to get for us . . . (*to girls*) . . . Now, what do we want . . . three Ski yoghurts, one bottle nail varnish remover, three Mars bars (*turns to audience*) . . . well, put it this way, a list 'bout ten feet long. And at the end I signed it Al Capone alias Wild Willy alias Mandy Willis, Master Thief of The World . . . and they set off.

Choc/Pip/Skin   Easy, Easy, Easy!!

Exit Choc, Pip and Skin

Andrea (*to Mandy*)   Do you think they'll do it?

Andrea   No.

Mandy   Well then fool, 'course they won't. They'll get into Jackson's, take one look at the security camera next to the yoghurt freezer, one look at that list, and they'll be back. Sweating fear!! Come on, let's go down to the park.

Paula (*to audience*)   We've arranged to meet them in the park later. We spend some time playing. On the swings. (*mimes activities, running from one ride to another*)

Mandy (*to Andrea*)   Come on Andrea stand up like this, it's ace!

Andrea   I can't, I daren't! (*she gives instructions to move* *on*) On the rocking horse . . . (*they jump onto the 'horse'*)

Mandy   Whey, woah, whey! (*rocking wildly*)

Andrea   Mandy stop, it's hurting the bones in me bum!

Paula   On the roundabout . . . (*they run to the roundabout*)

Mandy   Shh! Sssh! Shh! Wheyoo! Standing on and pushing with one foot . . . (*they stand and push*)

Andrea   Mandy stop. I feel pukey.

Paula   It's getting dark, where are they? They said they'd meet us down here. I bet they've gone home instead.

Andrea   What if they did pinch that stuff?

Mandy   We'll eat it.

Paula   I bet they've gone home!

Mandy   Yeah.

Andrea   Shall we go? (*they leave the park*)

Mandy   Yeah. (*to audience*) Home. My house. It's on a street of terraced houses. Built after the war, they were supposed to be temporary but it's the 70s and they're still here. Mainly constructed of plasterboard, breeze blocks and six inch nails. And there's Mum's house, like a mansion in a camp site. Smothered in all manner of decoration. A white wheel from a cart nailed on the front wall above the kitchen window, hanging basket, milk box and token holder nailed in the porch. The garden infested with gnomes – stone, plastic, painted, or plain. A bird bath. All contained in a neat eight by eight foot patch of balding lawn. My mum's work. She thought we lived somewhere else, I think. . . . I opened the door.

Mr Willis appears

Mandy (*to Dad*)   Hi!

Dad   You'll be high in a minute; six foot high on the end of my bloody toe!

Mandy (*to audience*)   Ooooo he's angry. I must be late. It's okay though, I've put my watch back ten minutes just in case. And if that fails I've got a story prepared about leaving my cardigan at Paula's and having to go back for it. Dad's a big man with muscles like Brutus, and the strength of an ox. At this moment he seemed even bigger. A giant. He works a massive crane by the river that lifts ten tons of metal and swings it into a skip on the docks.

Mr Willis   Inside, you.

Mandy (*to audience*)   Now he pushes me towards the living room as if I was made of paper, my feet barely touch the ground. (*she opened the door*) I opened the living room door and the first thing I see is Mum. Red faced, wearing her curlers and carpet slippers, she must have been getting ready for work. (*Mrs Willis appears, shocked and upset*) She's crying, her pride has been seriously injured and when she speaks I know she's ashamed of me.

Mrs Willis (Mum)   Mandy, how could you do this to us? You've always had what you needed. We've tried to give you everything and this is how you repay us.

Mandy (*to audience*)   She starts crying again. Then I know what has happened. I clung to the hope that I was wrong and they'd only found out that we'd broken the head off the 'Capo di Monte' balloon seller and stuck it back on with Bostic. But no, I looked around the door (*Choc, Pip and Skin appear*)

27

and my worst fears are confirmed. I see my sisters, red with humiliation, sobbing loudly, mouths open, gurgling with fear. Dad seething with anger, shame and disbelief. (*Mr Jackson appears*) Last of all I see Mr Jackson of Jackson's Mini Market. I don't look at his face but at a piece of paper he's got in his hand. (*Mr Jackson places paper in Mr Willis's hand*) The list of items I wrote, bearing the legendary signature 'Al Capone alias Mandy Wilson'. (*Mr Jackson exits*) Of course, the younger ones will be forgiven because they don't know any better. But as for me, I was in charge. I'm eleven, and responsible. What on earth was I thinking of?! (*to everybody*) But Mum, it wasn't only me!

Mrs Willis (Mum)   Oh, so who was it then? I don't see Paula and Andrea written down here. Why does it always have to be you? God only knows what Andrea's parents think. They'll think we're a right pair, me and your dad, having a kid who sends her sisters out pinching.

Mandy (*to audience*)   Obviously this is not going to blow over very quickly. I reckoned on the punishment. Could it be a few rounds with the slipper on the back of the legs and probably two weeks without pocket money as well? I've really upset Mum, and Dad is shattered, but knowing him it will turn to anger now that Mr Jackson's left.

Paula (*to audience*)   Mr Jackson didn't stay long. He's a reasonable man and saw that the culprits were in capable hands. He talked to Mandy's dad in hushed tones saying things like, 'Well, I think they know they were wrong' and 'As far as I'm concerned it's forgotten.' Then they parted still friends, in an uncomfortable way. (*Dad turns back towards the audience*) He turned towards them with his leather soled carpet slippers in his hands.

Mandy (*to audience*) We knew what would follow – a lecture and a beating all rolled into one. Like this, I'll demonstrate with Paula: 'Don't' – smack – 'you' – smack – 'ever' – smack – 'do' – smack . . . get the idea?

Mr Willis (*to the girls*) We've done *everything* for you three, do you know that?

Choc Dad, we're sorry!

Mr Willis You will be.

Pip We won't do it again.

Mr Willis You're right there, you won't when I've finished with you.

Mrs Willis We've tried to give you everything.

Lights fade on family scene. Mandy now stands alone

Mandy (*to audience*) Mum started crying again. It's true, who knows how long it takes to pay off the hire purchase bills for all the Christmas presents? Or how many hours of overtime have to be done to pay for the annual week at Butlins? They're good to us. Money doesn't grow on trees you know, they have to work hard for it! All the treats and presents and days out go through my mind, and my punishment begins as a burden of guilt and regret came down on my shoulders. My heart sank and tears began to rise in my eyes as I saw the sad end to my life of joyous crime. Mandy Wilson, master-thief, foiled by a device of her own invention.

(END OF PLAY)

Foreshore

by Briony Binnie

Alone on a deserted beach Frog tries to get off with Melanie. Their alter-egos, Mel and Les, a bit like older brothers and sisters, make it increasingly difficult by constantly interfering and giving the wrong sort of advice. Throughout the course of this play the two alter-egos cannot hear or see each other: directing their comments always to their other 'halves', Melanie and Frog.

CAST

Frog A gauche, gawky, fifteen year old, obsessed with facts, fancies Melanie and wears jeans and T-shirts with rude slogans on them

Les Frog's alter-ego. A smooth, macho version of Frog, fancies himself. Dresses as Frog does, but more 'casual'

Melanie A straight forward, practical, fifteen year old, obsessed with Kevin but attracted to Frog. Wears jeans and T-shirts

Mel Melanie's alter-ego. A confident, glamorous version of Melanie. Easily bored, she dresses as Melanie does, but with more 'style'

Seaside sounds. Sound of bus coming, voices as they get off. Bus pulls away. Frog comes onstage, throwing his arms about, carrying a towel

Frog   Oh isn't it great! It's hot. It's dead sunny. Sea's blue as a dirty video. Sand's so . . . so sandy. [*sits*] Sky's all kind of there. (*lying back*) It's there.

He comes further on

Frog (*excited*)   God! It's bloody fan-tastic. Nobody's here. Why isn't there anybody kind of around?

Frog's 'other-half' Les, swaggers on smoothly

Les   This is it. This is *your* day. This is your life.

Frog   Shut up Les.

Les   Just think. After this, she'll be all yours. *Dying* for you.

Frog (*to himself*)   Les, you got a dirty mind.

Les   It's *your* mind, mate. I'm all yours.

Frog   Leave me alone. Get off me back.

Les moves away a bit. Frog moves forward

Frog (*whistles to Melanie*)   What you waiting for? Come on, it's bad. It's desert island ruddy discs. I never seen nothing like it. It's paradise. It's like the . . . Isle of *Man*! Come *on*.

Melanie (*from offstage, out of breath*)   I'm comin', I'm comin'.

Frog   Then you're not coming quick enough.

Melanie (*offstage*)   If you're going to prat about . . .

Frog   You got to see this to believe it, Melanie.

Melanie (*offstage*)   I'm trying to bloody see it.

Frog   Look over there. It's probably France. No, no. It'll be America.

Melanie, bedraggled, steaming, in jeans and T-shirt, limps on, carrying endless bags, baskets, beach things, towels, etc

Frog   I can see som'ing sparkling. It's shining. It'll be the Eiffel Tower. No, I know what . . . It'll be the Empire State Building. Come here, Melanie. Look over *there* . . . (*he points*)

Melanie (*still holding everything*)   Where, where?

Frog   There!

Mel   Is this it?

Melanie   I can't see nothing. (*drops bags*)

Frog   Uh! . . . You blind or what? There! It's looking at you.

Melanie   What, that? That rusty brown thing over there?

Frog   Yeah.

Melanie   It's a bloody steel can, you wazzock. It's nothing but an old oil drum.

Frog (*gets up*)   It's not. You don't get oil drums in the Pacific.

Melanie   That's not the Pacific. It's the Irish Channel. It's an *Irish* steel can. The most radioactive sea on earth.

Frog jumps back and covers his crotch, unseen by Melanie. He eases himself back to look like he never moved. Mel, Melanie's other half, saunters round wearing the same clothes as Melanie. She stands close to Melanie. Mel puts her hands on her hips, looking sexy

Mel For God's sake, if he says it's the Pacific Ocean it's the bloody Pacific Ocean!

Melanie (*catching on*) Oh yeah, I can see it *now*. Yeah. I can see the flag at the top, there's a little man waving (*she waves*) Woohoo!

Frog Who you wavin' to?

Mel and Melanie laugh

Les She's having us on, you pillock.

Frog She's never.

They both look out to sea, searching. Melanie looks around her

Melanie This the place you was calling out about? This it?

Mel God, look at it.

Melanie (*low*) Shh . . . I don't want no conscience with me today.

Mel Hard luck, you've got me. You've really done it now. Sea's nasty. It's not even green.

Melanie (*thinking*) Least we can sun bathe.

Mel A whole day of him. How on earth are we going to manage?

Melanie accidentally puts her foot down on dog muck. She lifts it up quickly, looks at her shoe, sniffs it, puts it down

Melanie Ugh . . .

Mel Can't go home now. There isn't a bus back for ages. I told you. I told you. You don't ever listen to me, your inner voice. I warned you, I . . .

Melanie Mel, belt up will you?

Mel Well, I only said . . . you're me, love, you're me.

Melanie I'm not listening.

Mel Ha, you gotta listen. I'm your other half, can't run away from *me*!

Melanie walks past Mel, Frog watches her unpack

Frog Right. Where's the sandwiches?

Melanie The what?!

Frog Sandwiches.

Melanie But you said you'd bring them.

Frog You mean you haven't brought our sandwiches?

Melanie squawks, mouths, can't speak, looks at Mel

Frog We arranged it! Spam and pickle, you were going to do your corned beef and cucumber. Tomato and cheese. Egg. All yellow and kind of mmmm . . .

Mel (*to Melanie, pointing at Frog and laughing*) *Told* you!

Les (*to Frog*) You tell her. Go on. Tell her, tell her about the bus.

Melanie Oh no. *You* said 'Leave it to me, I'll do it'.

Frog (*taking Les' advice*) I looked up the bus times, me, I did.

Mel (*sarcastically to Melanie*) He looked up the bus times.

Melanie (*to Mel*) If I want your opinion I'll bloody ask for it.

Les (*to Frog*) Can't trust girls to do a bloomin' thing. Not even things they're supposed to do.

Melanie (*to Frog*) Is that all you think I'm good for? Making bleedin' sandwiches?

Les (*leering*) Oh no I don't.

Frog (*imitating Les*) Oh no I don't. (*does double-take*) No, no. No.

Melanie slams off to one side. Frog goes to explain

Les (*to Frog*) Don't run after her, lad.

Frog Honest, Melanie, I don't.

Melanie Okay. What'm I good for? If I'm not good for that, what'd you ask me here for?

Frog (*trying to get on good side of Melanie*) Well . . . you *are* good for that.

Melanie You just said I wasn't.

Frog You *are* good for that, you are.

Melanie For God's sake, Frog, make your mind up.

Mel Oh gosh, you pick 'em.

Les Let's see you get yourself out of this one then.

Melanie Go on.

Frog Go on what?

Melanie Forget it.

Frog Oh.

Melanie starts getting ready to sunbathe, finding a bikini in the bag. She gives it to Mel

Mel (*being difficult*)   What d'you want me to do with this?

Melanie   We're sunbathing, silly.

Melanie passes the towel to Mel and sorts out the bags. Meanwhile . . .

Frog (*gazing out to sea*)   Did you know that the world's largest sea's the South China Sea?

Melanie   Fancy that.

Mel (*shaking and laying out the towel*)   He's going to tell you all the ruddy facts of the South China Sea now.

Frog   It's got an area of one million, one hundred and forty-eight thousand, five hundred kilometres, squared. No, I tell a lie. Miles squared. Because in kilometres, it's two million, nine hundred and seventy-four thousand, six hundred kilometres squared.

Les (*to Frog*)   Go on. You're impressing her.

Mel (*to Melanie*)   I think he's trying to impress us.

Frog   Now the largest *gulf* in the world is the Gulf of Mexico. With an area of five hundred and eighty thousand, three hundred miles squared. Which in kilometres is . . . one million, five hundred thousand kilometres squared. Or so. And shore line's three thousand, one hundred miles, which is four thousand, nine hundred and ninety kilometres. Which means you can fit (*he measures her by holding his hands up*) if you take half a metre per person, about, er, two million, four hundred and ninety-five thousand people in a kilometre.

Melanie Bloody hell, let's go.

Frog Where?

Melanie Gulf of Mexico.

Les You can't even get the facts straight.

Melanie (*working it out*) Hang on . . .

Les It's one and a half people per metre.

Frog (*confident*) She won't know.

Melanie . . . that's one and a half people per metre.

Les/Mel Hah! (*they flick their wrists making a clicking sound with their fingers*)

Melanie Hold this towel up for me will you? And if I catch you looking, there'll be trouble.

Frog (*panics*) How?

Mel (*covers her face*) God, he can't even hold a bloody towel up.

Melanie (*shows him*) Like this.

Frog holds towel up covering Melanie's top half. Mel passes her the bikini top. She turns her back to the audience, appears to struggle, does the bikini top up under her T-shirt

Les Now's your chance.

Frog Chance for what?

Les Seeing her curves!

Mel (*sensing*) He is going to look. You can tell. You can see.

Melanie He wouldn't.

Mel *Kevin* would've looked by now.

Melanie I'd have been fighting him off.

They laugh

Les   Look, for God's sake.

Frog (*looking out to sea*) Where? Where?

Les   Don't believe it!

Frog (*sneezes*)   Ouw-wouch!

He drops the towel. Melanie has her T-shirt half way over her head. Back to audience. She rescues the towel

Melanie   You sodding pervert!

Frog (*moving back fast*)   What d'you mean?

Les   *Us*?

Frog (*to Melanie*)   What's one of them?

Mel   Told you.

Frog (*to Les*)   What's one of them?

Les   They'd trust us in a school of vestal virgins.

Mel   They'd trust *him* in a school of vestal virgins.

Melanie has now done up her bikini top. She sits on her towel and tries to get her jeans off, bikini bottoms on underneath

Melanie   Would you pull me jeans off?

Frog (*shocked*)   'Course I wouldn't. What'd you take me for?

Les   Say no.

Frog (*resolutely*)   No.

Mel   Spell it out for him.

Melanie   Would you please help me pull my jeans off. (*explaining*) Off of my feet.

40

Les She's asking you.

Frog How?

Melanie Here.

They struggle with the tight jeans which are caught around her ankles

Les Go on, go on, get her.

Mel (*to Les*) What'd you say?

Les Didn't know you could hear.

Mel (*to Les*) You dirty-minded slob.

Frog (*to Les*) What do I do?

Les Talk. Talk your way in.

Frog (*using his hands, trying not to look at her, babbling*) The largest bay in the world, if you measure it from end to end . . .

Les keeps trying to interrupt

Frog . . . I mean if you go where it's the kind of beginning of the sand, starting at where the end of the sands ends, I mean, you're walking dead straight, but 'course it couldn't be straight, it's Hudson . . .

Melanie (*amused*) Hudson who?

Les Oh my God, not that kind of talk you idiot.

Frog Hudson Bay.

Mel He's at it again. Who's he think he is? Norris-Mac-bleedin-Whirter?

Mel takes off T-shirt and jeans, bikini on underneath

Frog   Which is in northern Canada . . . (*he peters out, holding her jeans in his hand, absent-minded, turning them the right side out*)

Melanie whips jeans off Frog, lays out her towel, gets out a copy of Pride and Prejudice, *lies on her front, reads. Mel does the same*

Les (*to Frog*)   Well come on. Get your trousers down!

Frog (*holds his trousers*) I . . . what!

Les   Like this.

Les smoothly steps out of his jeans, trunks on underneath

Frog (*takes off his shoes*)   You mean (*trying to be smooth, with a flourish, he gets one leg out*) . . . But maybe she won't like my legs? (*tries to hide them*)

Les (*looking at his own*)   They're not bad.

Frog   Sometimes you get some dead hairy ones. All skin and bone. With kind of . . . ugly knees. Bunions on toes.

Les   Don't talk so daft. Legs aren't like that.

Frog (*gaining confidence*)   Yuh. See what you mean. They're pretty good legs.

Frog struts, admiring his legs

Les   Uuuugggghhh! (*pointing*) What the hell's *that*?

Frog   What? Where? How?

Les   There!

Frog   Where?

Les   That purply scar. It's got *things* growing out of it.

Frog (*relieved*) They're only hairs.

Les You can't get hairs growing out of scars.

Frog Oh my God (*tries to cover his legs and trousers, picks up shoes*)

Les How the hell did we get that one?

Frog Bus driver pushed me off the bus. He said I was fourteen. I never said I was fourteen.

Les You said you were thirteen.

Frog (*accusing*) And who suggested it?

Les He must've pushed us off pretty hard. I'd forgotten about that. No wonder there's so many complaints about violence on the buses.

Frog (*to himself*) I didn't mean it to be like this. I wanted . . . I wanted it to be sort of . . . kind of . . . Well, just . . . different. (*drops shoes and jeans*) Like I'd be . . . *tough*. Hard. She'd . . . admire my body. (*he exercises his muscles*) And there'd be no purple scars. I'd be all . . . real . . . (*dreaming*)

Frog and Les both sit, elbows on knees, looking out to sea, lights fade up on the girls

Melanie (*they stop reading*) I didn't want it to be like this . . . (*pause*) I wanted it to be . . . glamorous!

Mel Him to bring us here in his car . . .

Melanie Didn't even have the bus fare.

Mel . . . and keep saying 'I love you' . . .

Melanie Instead of Hudson's ruddy Bay.

Mel . . . and buying cocktails. Like Buck's Fizz. And Malibou, Margaritas. Pina Colada. And anything with . . .

Melanie and Mel (*together*) . . . Creme de menthe.

Melanie Instead of forgetting the sandwiches. Toma–to and cheese. Ham and pickle. And his stupid yellow eggs. (*Mel and Melanie sit up, look out to audience*) I'd strut around . . . (*Mel gets up, struts around*) And he would watch me (*Mel looks at Les*) with burning eyes. (*Les looks at Mel*) Waiting . . . with baited breath!

Les (*turns to audience, exaggerating*) Burning! (*pause*) Breath, baited!

Melanie He'd lay out a towel for me.

Les does so with a flourish

Melanie Arrange the sand underneath it.

Les smoothes out the wrinkles. Mel watches, sits on the towel

Melanie He'd say, 'I like your legs'.

Les (*to Mel*) I like your legs.

Melanie Then he'd ask if I wanted any cream putting on my back.

Les (*to Mel*) Can I put some cream on your back?

Melanie Then I'd reply:

Mel (*to Les*) Don't mind if you do.

Melanie And he'd rub it all kind of sensually.

Les does this crouching near her

Les (*to Mel*) You got a really curvy back.

Mel (*to Les*) Oh thank you. People say it's my greatest asset.

Les Oh no. I wouldn't say that. I'd say your greatest asset was your . . .

Mel (*sticks out prominent places*) Yes, yes?

Les . . . your feet.

Mel My what?!

Melanie mirrors Mel's surprise

Les Your feet. Lots of girls have dead hairy, smelly feet. With kind of *bumps*. Ingrowing toe nails. And their heels all . . . scabby. And blue. And on the bottom there's green. Green! I even knew a girl with a mole on the bottom of her foot . . . But, oh no, *yours* are nice feet.

Melanie Oh God no. No, he wouldn't say that. My feet! (*looking at her feet*) Jesus!

Frog Trouble with girls is . . .

Les (*stands by Frog*) They haven't learnt how to be men.

Frog They take hours making themselves look pretty then they won't let us touch them.

Les Because . . .

Frog 'You'll smear me make up'.

Les They wear jeans and high heels.

Frog And lurex socks.

Frog and Les Together!

Frog They listen to Peter Powell.

Les They join George Michael fan clubs.

Frog Or Julio Inglesias.

Les They stay in to watch Top of the Pops.

Frog And spend hours and hours criticising the dancers and 'adore' the bands.

Les They know all the words but they never know who's on drums.

Frog I'll tell you what you find round mountains of handbags . . .

Les Girls dancing . . .

Frog and Les . . . *With each other*!

Frog They spend hours on the phone talking to someone they saw five minutes ago.

Les They tell their mothers things.

Frog Then regret it.

Les They say 'There's nothing wrong'

Frog Or they say 'No, no, it doesn't matter'

Les All that mascara and black and blue stuff . . .

Frog Right down your favourite shirt you can't even trust your *mum* to wash.

Les They're bawling the make-up off on you that you couldn't even touch before hand. Then go and change their minds without warning you.

Frog Like not bringing the sandwiches.

Les Then they say it's your fault.

Frog They're all on diets.

Les They say they've got too much bulging here.

Frog And too little bulging there.

Les And if you agree, you're in for it.

Frog And if you don't, you're useless.

Les   'Cause you don't understand.

Frog (*pause*)   *I* don't understand! (*pause*) I pictured it, well, sort of hot. And kind of, well, *steamy*. Girls at my feet. With . . . *desire*.

Mel (*sits up*)   De–sire.

Frog   Admiring my every gesture.

Les stands by Mel, flexes his biceps

Frog   And my God she'd admire those muscles.

Frog crosses his arms, makes his hands bulge out his upper arms

Frog   I'd do my chest exercises and it wouldn't even hurt.

Both Les and Frog do the action

Frog   And she'd say, 'Oh my God . . .'

Mel (*to audience*)   'Oh my God . . .'

Frog   '. . . you've got just marvellous muscles.'

Mel   'You've got ever such sexy biceps.'

Frog   Then she'd swoon. Loving me.

Mel puts her arms round Les' legs

Mel   You're so . . . so . . .

Les   We could play with each other like Tarzan and Jane.

Les (*to Mel*)   Do you want to . . .

Mel (*to Les*)   Yes, yes?

Les   Play . . .

Mel   What?

Les unravels her arms, goes to lift, out an imaginary beach ball, throws it to her. She springs up, catches it, throws it back

Mel   Oh what a wonderful catch.

Les   Noo, that was a bad catch.

Mel   Are you in the team?

Les   (*modestly*)   Well, actually, I am. As it happens . . . (*pause*) I play for England.

Mel   Oh . . . fancy! You're my kind of man. (*looks at audience*)

Frog   (*picks up jeans*)   And then (*puts one leg in*) . . . and then (*another leg*) . . . I'd take her away. (*pulls up jeans*)

Les beats his chest, hooting Tarzan-fashion

Mel   Why do men have this obsession with Tarzan? (*picks up towel*) And guess who's got to play Jane?

Les   (*to Frog*)   Take her away? You would?! Well done. I'm teaching you something. Go on. Show her a bit of ball control.

Frog gets up, goes to stride over, his jeans are not properly fastened

Frog   D'you want to play ball . . . (*he falls*)

Melanie   What on earth you doing, Frog? Did you hurt yourself? You got to take your jeans off to sunbathe you know.

Frog   I was just going to ask you to play ball.

48

Melanie (*laughs*)   You can't play ball with your trousers round your ankles.

Frog   Well, I had thought of taking them off.

She goes to help him pull them off. They look at each other a moment, then break away

Frog (*embarrassed*)   Have you got anything to eat, Melanie?

Melanie (*embarrassed*)   It was you, remember, supposed to bring sandwiches.

Frog (*points to bags*)   What's in all those, then?

Melanie   Oh, this and that.

Frog   Like what and what?

Mel (*to Melanie*)   Don't let him see.

Les (*to Frog*)   What's she got?

Melanie (*evasive*)   Nothing that'd interest you.

Frog   Got any chocolate there?

Melanie   Yes, yes. Here you are. Have some. (*she hands it to him, he starts eating it*)

Mel (*to Melanie*)   It's *our* chocolate!

Les   It's her bloomin' chocolate!

Melanie   Well can I have some then?

Frog (*joking*)   Oh do have some chocolate . . .

Melanie (*takes it*)   Don't mind if I do!

Les (*to Frog*)   What ever's she got in there?

Frog   What have you got in that lot?

Melanie   Oh, stuff.

Frog Like what?

Mel (*to Melanie*) Hang on.

Melanie (*to Mel*) It's okay. (*to Frog*) There's nothing in here. (*starting to unpack*) Jumper.

Frog Why?

Melanie In case it rains. Another towel. A spare bikini. Sun glasses. Flippers. Mask. Snorkel and your old radio.

Frog (*putting on flippers*) These are good.

Melanie Don't do that, they're my brother's.

Mel (*to Melanie*) Mind out.

Melanie Why?

Mel There's a photo of Kevin in there.

Melanie Oh! (*starts trying to get things back in bag*)

Frog How d'you *walk* in these?

Les (*to Frog*) She's hiding something.

Mel (*to Melanie*) You sure it's hidden now?

Les What *is* it?

Frog (*ignoring him*) Don't you think it suits me?

Melanie Yes.

Frog (*adopts James Bond pose*) James Bond . . .?

Melanie You look terrific.

Les You look really stupid.

Frog Do I? Do I look terrific?

Mel They pay people to take things like him away in corporation dust carts.

Melanie   Get them off.

Frog falls over, trying to pull things off. He hands flippers to Melanie

Melanie (*looking at him*)   You're burning up!

Les (*to Frog*)   Act cool.

Frog (*to Les*)   How can I act cool when I'm burning up?

Melanie   Here. (*gives him some cream*)

Frog   Thanks.

Frog struggles out of his T-shirt, gets bottle caught up in the arm hole. Squirts cream all over himself. Still struggles

Frog   Oh God . . .

Mel (*to Melanie*)   I bet his Mum still undresses him at night.

Frog (*desperate to change subject. Grabs radio*)   Hey! D'you want to hear my radio? It's really good, I won it years ago in a competition. You had to complete a slogan tiebreaker thing. I put 'Make Your Arm Pit Your Charm Pit' . . . for a deodorant. (*looking at Melanie's blank face*) I didn't think it was very funny either. I copied it out of a book. But they must've liked it 'cause there were hundreds and thousands of entries. It takes baby 1.5v high performance batteries. And my goodness its performance is high. Sometimes there's a funny sort of crackling noise at about 7 pm on a Sunday night – but it's just after the charts so that's all right.

He turns it on with a flourish. Nothing. He rattles it, looks at Les, looks at audience

Mel   High performance my foot.

Les (*to Frog*)   Maybe the fact that you left it on all night might have something to do with it.

Frog   (*to Les*) Why's nothing going *right*?

Melanie   Come on! Let's *do* something. I know . . .

Mel   You're gonna have to do *something* or the day's going to end up a complete disaster.

Melanie   . . . let's go swimming.

Frog (*pause*)   Where?

Melanie   When you come to the seaside you sunbathe. You have a picnic . . . you build sandcastles and you swim. In the sea.

Frog   I'm just in the mood to build a sandcastle.

Melanie   We're going swimming.

Frog   Let's just go paddling.

Les (*to Frog*)   You must be joking.

Frog (*finding an excuse*)   It's not just oil drums in there you know. There's Mersey Docks and Harbour Boards' cack in there.

Melanie   I can't see any.

Les   Don't tell her.

Frog   Did you know . . .

Mel   Here we go.

Frog   . . . in London, they re-use the water fourteen times.

Melanie   That's never true.

Frog   It is. When I went to my Aunt Isabel's in

52

London, I saw *things* floating in it. Not to mention the rubbish.

Melanie What rubbish?

Frog Told you not to mention it! And I could tell they were re-using it, 'cause it *tastes*.

Melanie What of?

Frog Well, at one end of the street, it's quite weak chlorine but at the other end, it's . . . strong.

Melanie That's not true. I happen to *know* that's not true.

Frog How?

Melanie Common sense. I done it in Biology.

Mel Go on educate him.

Melanie There's a circle. It's ecology. It gets purified by the salt. And the sun evaporates it. It falls as rain and we drink it. It goes round and round and round.

Frog Like the Earth. (*they look at each other*)

Melanie Come on. Let's go swimming.

She grabs Frog by the hand. Blue and rippling lights shimmer as they move towards the sea

Les For heaven's sake, don't tell her you can't swim.

Frog (*backing off*) Look, em, I'm not dead good at swimming.

Mel He can't swim. That'll be why they call him 'Frog'.

Melanie We don't have to swim. We can jump. You lose as many calories jumping as swimming. Come on, come on, get ready . . . jump!

The girls jump together eagerly. The boys half-heartedly

Melanie I can feel yesterday's tea burning off me!

They jump

Frog Lucky we didn't have those sandwiches. That'd be a hundred more jumps.

They jump

Les I do feel a prat.

Melanie (*shouts*) Let's go deeper.

Boys jump back. Girls jump forward. Sound of waves increase with the scene

Melanie (*shouts*) If I jump higher and deeper, that's today's dinner and tomorrow's breakfast gone!

Les and Frog remain shivering at the water's edge

Frog What's the point of eating if you got to jump it off afterwards?

Melanie (*jumps*) Monday's éclair. (*jumps*) Wednesday's Eccles cake. (*very high*) And that doughnut I had.

Frog and Les move back, watching

Frog She forgot . . .

Les (*interrupting*) She forgot the sandwiches, on purpose!

Melanie Oh, I do love it when there's extra big waves and they go all over you and it's cool and refreshing.

The girls kick and splash in the sea

Frog It's bloomin' freezing. There's parts of me so cold they're going to fall off.

Melanie (*kicking water at Frog and Les*) It's ace. It's great. I'm glad we came.

Les (*looking at Mel*) She doesn't look that bad when she's smiling and laughing.

Mel (*to audience*) What d'you mean? I always look good.

Frog (*proudly, looking at Melanie*) I did right to bring her here.

Mel It's so good when you really are enjoying yourself. When you're hot and then cold and then boiling hot and then cool. And you feel you're going to burst.

Frog (*teeth chattering, hugging himself*) I don't really feel too good. There's things swimming round your feet. You're jumping on them and killing them. And it's you who was all upset about ruining the system.

Melanie (*yells*) The system loves me!

Frog (*low*) There's neo-pilina in there. There's flat worms. There's the floating larva of the bracheopods. Miss Wilson told me in Lower 2B. There's sea slugs. There'll be scallops getting in the hairs on your legs. There's all kinds of molluscs.

Melanie slows down, peers about

Frog There's nautiluses, could even be nautili, there's squids. There's star fishes – star fish-i. There's giant clams and other bi-valves. At your feet.

Melanie But I can't see nothing.

Frog Just 'cause you can't *see* them doesn't mean they're not *there*.

Melanie Where?

Frog It's much more fun building sandcastles.

Mel (*looks at Les*) Let's get dry, Melanie. (*moves upstage to get towel, Les looks over to her, and crouches, looking out to sea*)

Lights back to sunshine, wave sounds quieter

Melanie My skin's all tingly. I can imagine my blood vessels contracting and dilating all over the place. (*to Frog*) What gets *you* like that?

Frog Watching Dalglish and Ian Rush in action or McDermott in the box.

Melanie groans. Goes to pick up towel and dries herself

Les (*moves to Frog*) That's true. When that ball just misses the goalie and cuts through the air and squeezes into that little net, makes me go . . . puuuuur-chung inside ready to burst.

Melanie Is that why whole lines of fans go up and down in their seats, like yo-yos?

Girls laugh

Frog That's right.

Frog and Les dry themselves and begin to dress. Frog watches Melanie

Mel (*to audience*) It's as though there's a glass wall between us. Sometimes when you feel so good and on top of the world, because they don't feel like that, you're alone, nobody else is sharing your happiness – that's what makes the wall. It separates you, cuts you off, making some of your happiness turn. (*Mel holds towel up for Melanie. She puts T-shirt and jeans on behind towel.*)

Les (*to Frog*) Look. Look at that.

Frog No.

Les Why not? Doesn't hurt.

Frog 's bad.

Les For goodness sake we've spent all morning wishing she'd do that, now's the chance.

Frog (*weakening*) Supposing she catches me looking?

Les How can she catch you looking when she's struggling with a towel?

Frog I wonder what would happen if she did see me. Les, what'd she think of me?

Les She'd love you for it.

Frog It's not a very gentlemanly thing to do.

Les Stuff 'gentlemanly'. Half the time they want you to be all chivalrous and restrained and the other half they want you to be all macho and sex machine.

Frog Does she want me to look?

Les 'Course she does.

Melanie (*turning round*) Don't you look. You put a bloke in a position of trust and honour and he abuses it. Typical.

Mel Something has to ruin it.

Frog   Oo, I'm not, I was looking at that thing behind you there.

Melanie (*looks*)   There's nothing behind me.

Mel   Typical. Of the lot of them.

Frog (*changes subject*)   This is good sandcastle sand. It's all fine and shimmering. Waiting for someone to come and make a castle. (*he gets down on his hands and knees to build a castle. Melanie picks up her book. She listens to Frog.*)

Frog   And we'll use lollipop sticks for flagpoles and masts. . . . And the shells'll make a pathway up to the castle. . . . I could make anything with these. Anything I wanted . . .

Les (*joins in*)   What do you think it would feel like if these grains were people and *you'd* got control over them?

Frog   Nobody can have control over people because people can think. (*he squats, looks out to sea*) It takes one man . . .

Mel (*from behind her book*) . . . or woman.

Frog   . . . to change the system.

Melanie (*she moves close and squats by him*)   You're right and it's bad when you can see it's all wrong but you can't do a thing about it. When I get down, I think about the one in three or whatever it was getting killed by The Plague and nothing's as bad as that. It was in one of my history books. But the sand goes on and on being made so slowly. It's always there. (*pushes him down. They laugh*) If *that* doesn't cheer me up I go and eat a cream cake.

Frog (*looks at book*)   What book are you reading?

Melanie Oh it's great. I'm reading it for school. We were supposed to hand in an essay last Friday. I haven't even finished it yet. It's about these families, they're kind of rivals. There're these two men, right, and one of them's useless and the other's all right. And the one that's useless turns out all right and the one that's all right, turns out to be a real prat. The good one's called D'Arcy – he's bad, bad. And Wickham's such a jerk. And the girls are all flowing. Going to balls and all. And having faints. And they have carriages, and servants. Wish it was still like that.

Frog (*identifying with the jerk*) Like that?! You're joking. It's rubbish. That's what it is. That's the sort of rot people fall for. Who wrote it anyway?

Melanie Jane Austen.

Frog (*looks at Les*) Is that Austen Motors? (*laughs*)

Melanie You're so unromantic. It's not just the dresses, it looks nice. It's a nice idea. They had these coats with big collars, black and grey and tall hats and that. And shirts with frills, and . . .

Frog Frills, huh. Were they all poofs, or what? (*looks at Les*)

Melanie (*angry*) You're so stupid. You're so scared of being thought effeminate.

Mel (*moving in. Frog is caught between them*) They were dead classy. You're so scruffy.

Melanie You should have seen the trousers they used to wear. Cream or grey. Straight.

Mel Tight, close fitting.

Frog But I wear 'em straight.

Melanie You don't know what I'm on about.

Mel You like T-shirts with rude slogans on them and your trousers have been let down twice.

Melanie Even three times, and they're still too short.

Mel And you only ever clean your shoes on the backs of your jeans, and when was the last time you changed your socks? And I'll tell you the worst thing.

Melanie It's when you carry on wearing your summer clothes in the middle of winter . . .

Mel . . . and pretend you're not dead frozen.

Melanie . . . and we can all see your goose pimples up your arms and even inside your stupid ears.

Mel Go on. You tell him.

Les (*desperate*) Don't stand for that.

Frog But she's right.

Melanie And you're so illiterate.

Mel All you read is the latest science fiction.

Melanie Or rubbish like *The Revenge of the Rats*!!

Mel All guts and gunge.

Melanie And tell me your favourite magazine. Go on.

Mel It'll be *Exchange and Mart*. His mother probably picked him up there in exchange for his father.

Les (*desperate, to Frog*) Don't cock it up, say *Playboy* or *Knave*.

Frog *Exchange and Mart*.

Mel Told you.

Melanie And you love those stupid music papers with those long words you can't understand.

Mel   Love repeating them.

Melanie   And you listen to such *crap*.

Mel   It's all Electro . . .!

Melanie   And the more you think you like it, more it sounds like a ten ton lorry.

Mel   With brake failure.

Melanie   Towing a tank.

Frog   Oh no, I do like . . .

Les   Go on, think of someone.

Mel   Ask him.

Melanie   Who do you like then?

Les   Tell her who we went to see.

Frog   Run DMC.

The girls slap hands

Mel   All yours.

Melanie   I'll tell you what I heard about that concert. You were all so busy fighting round the back you never even saw the nurds playing. Well, 'course, they weren't playing. They were rolling about on stage making your ears bleed. And most of you were stoned. For a treat you like mixing sherry and guinness and seeing how long you can stay standing. And when you're dead refined you drink Pomagne from the bottle and ask one of us to dance. And all we can hear in our ears is these sweet nothings, . . . burp, burp, burp. And we're supposed to be grateful.

Mel (*enjoying this*)   Go for it, go for him.

Les   Show her who's boss. This is out of order.

Frog   Wait on.

Melanie Wait for what?

Mel Now's your big chance. Walk out on him.

The alter-egos confront one another

Les (*to Mel*) You can't. There's no buses for hours.

Mel (*to Les*) Keep your big nose out of this business.

Les This *is* my business, you!

Mel Who asked you along?

Les I *am* him. If you get him, you get me.

Mel But we don't want either of you. We only came along to make your best friend jealous.

Melanie (*to Mel*) Now that isn't true.

Les (to Frog) I don't know why you're interested in her. She's just using you.

Frog (*to Les*) No that isn't true.

Frog and Melanie now face each other.

Les You know damn well it's true.

Melanie Frog, I'm sorry. I thought that at first, but . . . I prefer you to Kevin, you've got more to say for yourself.

Frog (*hurt*) You mean all this was for Kevin, to impress him? But he's not even *here*.

Melanie Look . . . Frog . . . How d'you get such a stupid name?

Frog (*repeats*) For *Kevin*?

Melanie What's your real name?

Les (*quickly*) Don't. Don't tell her.

Mel (*sarcastic*)   I bet it's Arthur or Claude or something.

Melanie   What is it?

Frog   Kevin's such a prat.

Les (*to Frog*)   Don't let it out you're called Lesley. She'll have a fit.

Mel (*to Melanie*)   Ask him if it's Lesley.

Melanie   Is it . . . Les?

Frog   Kevin *uses* girls. He just uses them. He picks them up and dumps 'em.

Les (*knowing he has blown it*)   Oh no!

Frog   Kevin'll wrap you round his little finger and just flick you away.

Melanie   It is, isn't it? You're called Les.

Frog (*shouts*)   And what if I am called Lesley? It's not my fault if my parents chose a stupid name. It's better than Darcy!

Mel   Lesley. What a name.

Melanie (*to Mel*)   And who asked you? You've caused enough trouble as it is. Keep out of it. He can't help his name.

Mel flounces away

Les   You shouldn't have told her about the name. (*walks to the other side*)

Frog   Melanie. (*pause*) Kevin may seem to be a good bloke but you should hear the things he says about girls.

Melanie (*looks at him*)   What things?

Frog He comes to school and boasts about the night before. What girl he's had. What he's done. And he's never very, well, kind of pleasant.

Melanie But he's your friend.

Frog Sure he's my friend – his dad's in videos. I'd be stupid not to have him as a friend. You've got such dead romantic ideas. And they're not even practical. You're just going for the *looks* of the thing, the outside. Not for what's inside (*moves towards her*) It's not frilly shirts or tight pants or hats or that. It's nothing to do with carriages or servants or fainting and all. As if that really matters! (*pause*) What *does* matter is what a bloke's like when nobody else is looking at him. When he's not posing. Not like on a Saturday night and he's all dressed up for the disco. You don't see *him* then. You're seeing his clothes.

Melanie (*loud*) I like his clothes. They're better than yours.

Frog (*low*) You should hear the things he says about you.

Melanie puts her head down, sits, curled up. Frog touches her shoulder. Les and Mel watch, amazed

Les Good grief.

Mel Body talk.

Frog (*straight out to audience*) Les, what do I do now?

Les Other arm. Round her.

Frog puts other arm round Melanie

Mel (*Melanie looks at audience*) It took him this long!

Les Kiss her, kiss her!

Frog (*to audience*) Where?

Les Where people *normally* kiss.

Frog kisses her ear

Mel (*brushing her ear*) I can't stand my ears being touched. (*Melanie looks at audience*)

Frog (*to audience*) I got a mouthful of hair.

Les Not there! On her mouth!

Mel (*to audience*) Why can't men (*Melanie turns and looks at audience too*) be smooth? He's going to say . . .

Frog . . . The longest kiss in a film is one hundred and eighty five seconds.

Mel (*smiles*) Show me! (*Melanie smiles*)

Les (*to Frog*) Move a little.

Frog But *where*?

Les To face her. Round.

Frog tries to work out what he's doing, tries to follow orders

Les Round!

Frog struggles round

Les More.

Frog struggles round more

Mel I hope his breath doesn't smell.

Frog Where's my nose go?

Les To the side, and not in her mouth . . .

*Mel and Les slap hands, and knock hips from the side.
Melanie closes her eyes, they are about to kiss. Sound of bus
coming. Frog stops. Frog moves away. Melanie still with
eyes closed, expecting to be kissed*

Frog It's the bus! Quick, get your stuff Melanie. I'll
run on and stop it.

*He runs off. Melanie starts collecting things up, drops things,
picks them up, drops others, exit running*

Melanie I'm coming, I'm coming!

Mel (*picking things up*) Days at the seaside aren't that
bad. It could've been the zoo. He could have told us
the mating habits of the lesser spotted orangutang.

Les I bet her Darcy would've known how to kiss. But
then his tight trousers would've stopped him.

Mel starts to walk out, the alter-egos exchange a look

Les Can I help you pick them up?

Mel drops something purposely. Les picks it up with a flourish

Les C'mon. They better not go without their consci-
ences. Heaven knows how he'd manage on the bus
. . . (*both exit, running*)

All (*offstage*) Wait on . . . hang on . . . hold on . . .
don't go . . . wait for us . . .

Sound of bus leaving. Seaside sounds.

(END OF PLAY)

Back Street Mammy

by Roselia John Baptiste

CAST

Innes West Indian middle-aged woman, with four children. Cafe owner, very independent

Mother Dynette's West Indian mother. Raised two children on her own

Jacko Middle-aged West Indian man, always in cafe. Clothes once fashionable, now scruffy. Drinker and gambler

Eddie West Indian cockney, 'Mr Cool' type. Aged about twenty-two

Dynette Sixteen year old black girl. Serious and quiet

Little Girl in park Under ten years

Woman offstage Eddie's new girlfriend

These extracts, taken from a full length play, shows one young woman's dilemma when faced with an unplanned pregnancy. Dynette is growing up, discovering her own sexuality and finding that she has little say in her future. In the original play, poetic verse linked various scenes, but has been omitted here for easier reading.

EXTRACT ONE

Dynette has left home in the middle of the night. She is sitting centre stage on a suitcase. Lights come up slowly.

Dynette I was fourteen, catching up on last year's fashion; borrowing my sister's stiletto heels and pencil skirts. Wore my first bra, elasticated, pink and pointed. Didn't feel shame to take off my vest in the swimming bath changing rooms any more. I received my first valentine card from the boy in Form 3A4 I had a crush on. I felt like a grown-up for the first time with heels and skirt and card. I prayed for three things: a tennis racket; a boyfriend; and my periods to start. I did exercises to increase my thirty inch chest. I pulled at my nipples, straightened my nose, my back, my hair. (*pause*) I followed my sister to parties, then blues. My first memory of blues is a van load of kids and boxes belonging to the 'Scorcher Sound System' arriving outside an old terraced house at two o'clock in the morning. Inside hot and dark, a blazing coal fire, ganja burning my eyes, my sister dancing with her fella, me standing there like a shadow. Nothing made sense then. I thought that by growing up fast I would find all the answers. I was naive. (*pause*) At fifteen school was fun. I was sure that I would pass my 'O' levels. I had a crush on my sister's boyfriend's friend. He was nice looking. Reminded me of a black version of **Clint Eastwood**. Cool. He bought me a drink, treated me like an adult. He said that I looked eighteen so I told him that I was. He made my finger tips tingle when he looked at me. I couldn't talk about it to anyone. (*pause*) Then it happened . . . really quickly. Whirlwind romance? No, not like the films or the books. No flowers, no chocolates, no roses, no champagne, just pure guess work really. The suspense of not knowing when I'd see him again. Sort of exciting. (*she touches the suitcase*) Made love for the first time at my sister Joy's party, when everybody had gone home. I 'relaxed on the settee' with Eddie. I'd dreamed about it so much, it just didn't feel real. He told me he loved me. (*pause*) Eddie left early before I woke up. I think I knew then that there would be no time to worry about whether he loved me or not. No doctor had to tell me that I was pregnant. I couldn't face my mother or my sister. I didn't know who to turn to so I packed my bags one night and sneaked out of the house.

EXTRACT TWO

An all-night West Indian cafe. Innes is dusting the counter. She puts up a blackboard with a list of West Indian food and prices. Patties, rice, chicken, curry goat, fritters, and fried dumpling. Jacko, in a battered Trilby hat and old raincoat, is sitting on a stool in the corner nursing a bottle of wine. Dynette enters carrying a suitcase and looking for Eddie, the father of her child. Jacko is singing, half-talking to himself. It is the middle of the night.

Jacko   Nex' time me gawn go meself. (*shakes his head and tuts. Then starts singing*)
Come in Abraham
Where you been so long?
Every time I turn on me bed
I take me pillow for you.
Nobody know

How dry we are
I sold me shoes
For a bottle of booze . . .

(*talking to himself*) Damn ITV Seven, me did need one
horse fe win, it nah even place. Damn raas boi gone
deaf and is me that have to pay for it. Nex' time me
gawn go meself . . . (*he notices Dynette*) You allright
girl? (*he giggles*) Me is an old man talking to meself,
never mind me. (*continues singing*)

Come in Abraham
Where you been so long?
Every time I turn on me bed
I take me pillow for you.
Nobody know
How dry we are
I sold me shoes
For a bottle of booze.

*Jacko continues to mutter and sing quietly. His eyes drift into
not seeing. Faded eyes. Worn face. Tired. Innes shakes her
head*

Innes   You still here Jacko, still arguing over that last
ten pound? Not going to do you no good you know.
You won't get it back by moaning.

Jacko   But me did tell 'im, Electra the horse that going
to win. Now if me never tell 'im it would be
different, but me did tell 'im, and 'im throw me
money away 'pon some General Nuttin horse me
never hear of. Nah even reach the firs' fence. Still, no
sense talking, no sense moaning ent it Innes? The
money gone so me mus' sing, nah true?

Innes   You want serving, girl?

Dynnette comes out of her daze

71

Dynette Two fritters please.

Innes Fritters done. All we have lef' is patty. You want patty?

Dynette Yes please . . . two.

Innes They not too hot and me not putting them back in there, so I hope you like cold patty. (*she hands them to Dynette*)

Dynette Thank you.

Innes (*to Jacko*) These young children don't know what to do with themselves these days. One o'clock in the morning and the child buying cold patty when it's in her bed she should be sleeping.

Jacko I would be a rich man now you know Innes, a rich man, if that raas boi had done me message right.

Innes (*sighs*) Jacko, you were born to be Jacko and no matter what message you give you will always be . . .

Jacko (*interrupts*) Jacko, I know, but you have to take a chance, try a likkle ting else you get nowhere, ent it? You have to. Ax de chil'. What you say? (*Dynette looks at him blankly*) Girl, you look in a bad way you know. You leave home nah? Where you going at this time of night wid suitcase? (*Dynette looks at the suitcase*)

Innes (*kissing her teeth*) Damn nasty children is, so they is. When 'is time for them to help de modder in de house, 'is so they doing just packing their clothes and playing big woman. Damn laziness.

Jacko Leave de chil' woman, let she talk. (*to Dynette*) You leave home for true?

Dynette I'm looking for Eddie Thomas

Innes   Eddie . . . (*to Jacko*) Not the one you does walk wid sometimes?

Jacko   Whatever he do to you girl it mus' be bad because dat look in your eye ain't nice. It look like trouble to me. Any woman travel the night wid suitcase come look for me, me sure she ain't gawn find me. No me nah think 'im gawn come in here tonight because if me catch him wid me ten pound bet, 'im gawn mess up, me gawn kill 'im. 'Is Eddie you love sick for girl? Then you mus' go find yourself another man for that one pass caring for.

Innes   Girl, why you don't go home to your bed and sleep? You don't have to go school tomorrow? You must be no more than fifteen. Your modder gawn box you for make her worry so. You mussa argue en it? You mussa argue about de boi you gawn follow. But dat boi Eddie Thomas is no good. 'Im have enough girl follow 'im. Go 'ome to your modder girl. (*pause*) Come. (*she clasps Dynette close*) I have children too, you know girl. I know how your mammy mus' be feeling. She mus' talk, she mus' say a few things but take no mind to what she say tonight, tomorrow things make more sense.

EXTRACT THREE

Eddies house. Dynette pauses, uncertain for a moment then knocks at the door

Eddie (*offstage*)   Who's that?

A woman's laughter is heard offstage. It is Eddie's new girlfriend

Dynette   Eddie is that you?

Eddie   Who is it cha?

73

Dynette Me . . . Dynette.

Eddie Who?

Dynette Open the door it's important.

Eddie, towel around his waist, half opens the door

Eddie What are you doing here?

Dynette I've been looking for you all night. I've got to talk to you.

Woman's voice (*offstage*) Who's there Eddie?

Eddie (*to Dynette*) Do you know what you're doing?

Dynette Stop treating me like a child. I wouldn't be here if it wasn't important.

Eddie steps out of the house and tries to make himself look more respectable by putting on his hat. He stands closer to Dynette, speaks softly, moving them both away from the door

Eddie What is it?

Dynette I'm pregnant.

Eddie Who for? . . . (*recollecting*) . . . not for the one time we did a likkle ting. Look girl, I'm not in the mood for joking and if it's not a joke, well then, you've got the wrong man.

Dynette There hasn't been anyone else, you *know* you were the first man I slept with. I told you, remember?

Eddie That's your story.

Dynette It's true.

Eddie Look, why me? Can't you pick on someone else? You're still at school. I could be put away for that.

Dynette Amongst other things.

Eddie What do you mean by that?

Dynette I don't know Eddie, I don't know, I don't even know what I'm doing here. All I know is I'm pregnant and my mum will kill me when she finds out.

Woman's voice (*offstage*) Eddie . . .

Eddie (*to himself*) But look a predicament me Eddie Thomas find meself in. This multiplication business is moving too fast for me. The thought of likkle miniature Eddies running wild in dis rat trap is not what I want. There's nothing I have done that I'm proud enough to pass on to me pikni dem. I'm only just surviving . . . selling a likkle draw to line me pocket . . . cha the girl lie, man . . . some bredrin go mess wid her and is me, soft-hearted Eddie, go pay for it . . . (*to Dynette*) Look, meet me in the park tomorrow at three. I'll get some money together and we'll sort this thing out. Right now I've got to get some . . . sleep.

Woman's voice (*offstage*) Eddie, you not coming?

Eddie (*to Dynette*) You know how it is.

Dynette I haven't got anywhere to stay.

Eddie Go home girl, go home. Your mum will never know, just go home and forget the whole thing. Meet me tomorrow and I promise everything will be all right.

75

Eddie goes inside, shuts the door. Dynette stands outside his house as the lights go down

EXTRACT FOUR

The next day. Dynette is sitting. Her mother is plaiting her hair

Mother When I finish with your hair you make a start with the plate. (*Dynette is not listening*) You hear what I'm saying Dynette?

Dynette What . . .?

Mother Who you saying what? You think you is big woman you can just answer me anyhow? Have no respect.

Dynette I didn't hear what you said.

Mother No, your mind jus' a drift like you have all the world problem on your head. Where your mind is? When 'is study, you should study to pass at school, 'is *man* you a study.

Dynette MAM!

Mother W' happen? You don't like to hear the truth?

Dynette looks at her mother with disgust

Dynette Have you nearly finished?

Mother Why? You in a hurry to go somewhere? I tell you to wash the plate before you go anywhere, you know. You have no time these days to spend a little time wid your modder. You jus' a waste your life.

Dynette Oh mam.

Mother The plate.

Dynette (*standing up*) I'll do them when I come back. I've got to go somewhere.

She leaves

Mother (*shouts*) Dynette!!

Lights down

EXTRACT FIVE

Dynette is sitting in the park waiting for Eddie. He's late

Dynette Summer day. Kids laughing, skipping, eating ice cream. The sound of radios, murmurs . . . slow cricket matches, speeding wasps, buttercups. Lift up your chin and I'll tell you whether you like butter or not. Daisy chains for jewellery. He loves me he loves me not. Blowing dandelions to tell the time. One o'clock, two o'clock . . .

Looks at her watch and looks around to see if Eddie has arrived

Little girl (*enters skipping with rope, singing*)
Bluebells cockle shells
Eevory Ivory over

Dynette jumps with her. Little girl continues singing

Oh Dynette I'm telling your mother
For kissing Eddie Thomas in the parlour
How many kisses did you give him?
One, two, three, four . . .

Eddie approaches. When Dynette notices him the game stops. Little girl looks at him, looks at her, then runs off skipping

Eddie So you come a woman?

Dynette Didn't think you'd come.

Eddie Of course I'd come, I'm here aren't I? Couldn't keep a pretty girl like you waiting.

Dynette You're already half an hour late.

Eddie Cha . . . I reach. So you want to talk about this child business.

Dynette There's nothing to talk about.

Eddie So why you search half the night for me . . . not through love alone?

Dynette I'm pregnant Eddie, pregnant . . .

Eddie Twice! I hope it's by the same guy. (*he laughs, Dynette looks away*) Don't get heated up sister, what you expect? (*pause as Eddie listens, then sings along with an ice cream van*) I'm Popeye the sailor man and I live in . . . hey babes you want ice cream? Pop ice? (*pause*) Me nah do nuttin wrong you know, we have me spar Leeroi to voice for me. Leeroi was there when you tell me your age. You think I would mess with a school girl? Spoil my image. (*eyes her*) Still you all right you know, 'can't blame you for trying.

Dynette turns to go. Eddie grabs her arm seriously, aggressively. He puts a wad of notes under her nose

Eddie I want you to get rid of it. I don't want to hear no more from you or anyone else about your belly ache right?

Dynette looks at the money for an instant then at Eddie. She snatches the money. Lights come down as Eddie exits. Spot light on Dynette holding money

Dynette I'd never really thought about the alterna-

78

tive. I'd automatically thought that I would keep the baby, but I couldn't sleep at night worrying. I was feeling sick all the time . . . throwing away my studies. It panicked me. I just couldn't think straight. I tried to figure out the best way to tell Mum. She wouldn't understand. She'd think straight away of child maintenance and court cases. I didn't want any of that. I thought I'd go mad. I thought it over and over. I signed the papers that told me I would be at risk if I were to continue with the pregnancy. It hurt — signing — I felt empty. I needed to talk to someone. To the doctors I was just a number. I didn't know of anyone who could have possibly understood. So I kept my secret.

(END OF PLAY)

Dead Proud

by Angie Milan

CAST

Lesley Nearly sixteen, bored with school, desperate to leave home and in love with Orlando

Orlando Half-Spanish. Couple of years older than Lesley. Likes motorbikes

Maggie Lesley's mum. Thirty-six and needs a break

Isobel Lesley's mate. Sixteen, Jamaican and fancies Jimmy. Still lives at home, with her one-year-old son

Lesley Orlando is half-Spanish. He's got deep brown
eyes – they look right through you. He'd catch me
eye at the youth-club, made me go all tingly inside.
(*pause*) When he wanted a bit – I always knew – we'd
go round his mum's after club. She'd go upstairs to
bed and make a load of noise, reminding us she was
awake. Didn't make any difference though.

Orlando Lesley . . . what a mover, fell in love with
her on the dance floor. Great sense of humour, I like a
girl with a sense of humour. And active, very active,
if you know what I mean. (*pause*) Best bit is getting
ready to meet her. Bathing, washing me hair, ironing
me shirt, shaving, splashing it all over – knowing that
Les would be kissing it all off two hours later.

EXTRACT ONE

*Two months later they split. Two months after that Lesley
discovers she's pregnant. She tells Orlando hoping he will
whisk her off her feet, marry her, and then live happily ever
after. Orlando has other ideas, he is 'going places' and
doesn't want to have anything to do with Lesley or the
child. Lesley is determined to keep the baby.*

★

*At Lesley's home. The living room – very cramped. Too
much furniture, magazines, food packets, toys etc. Lesley's
mother Maggie holds a dust-pan and brush and is listening
to the radio which is blasting out Radio London (Tony
Blackburn). Listening and brushing up mess on the floor,
she shifts the rubbish around to no effect. Lesley enters,
turns down radio.*

Maggie Here, I was listening. It's 'Listen with Love'
next. (*turns it up again*)

Lesley (*turns it down*) Mum, I'm two months over . . .

Maggie Me only chance for a bit of romance.

Lesley . . . with me period.

Maggie You're only young, happens all the time. I shouldn't worry.

Lesley I know I'm pregnant.

Maggie (*speechless*) Well. (*long pause*)

Lesley Mum. Say something.

Maggie I'm finished.

Lesley Sorry.

Maggie Jesus.

Lesley Said I was sorry.

Maggie What will your father say?

Lesley Dunno.

Maggie You bitch, you stupid little bitch.

Lesley It ain't as bad as that.

Maggie You don't know what you're saying.

Lesley You went with Dad before you got married.

Maggie And look where I've ended up. How dare you do it without telling me.

Lesley I can't tell you them things.

Maggie You could have at least used a bleedin' durex.

Lesley I don't like them.

Maggie So you've had it often enough to know. Are you sure? You might be nervous or something.

Lesley I've had one of them tests, cost me five quid.

Maggie Where'd you get five pounds from? Prostituting yourself I suppose.

Lesley I'm no bleedin' prostitute.

Maggie Pregnant at fifteen.

Lesley I borrowed it from Isobel.

Maggie You told her before your own mother?!

Lesley She's me best mate.

Maggie And I don't matter.

Lesley I was frightened.

Maggie Frightened? (*pause*) Where did she get five pounds from? 'Suppose she prostitutes herself as well.

Lesley (*getting angry*) She got it from her mother.

Maggie So her mother knows. Shaming me like this and me not knowing . . . Always been selfish you have, don't think of anyone else . . . (*cries*) . . . Going to someone else's mother . . . a stranger . . . What they must think of me.

Lesley At least she understands.

Maggie And I don't. (*Lesley goes to leave*) Where do you think you're going?

Lesley Going out.

Maggie You stay here madam. (*paces around*) How many months?

Lesley Two.

Maggie Well, you can have it out.

Lesley I ain't having it out, it ain't a bleedin' tooth.

Maggie You are *not* having this kid, you're too young.

Lesley It ain't yours to give away.

Maggie You're dead right it ain't. Soon as you've had it, you're out. What about the father. Who is he?

Lesley What do you care?

Maggie Heaven forbid if he was black. We can't have no black baby in this family. Your father won't allow it.

Lesley You don't understand. The baby is *mine*.

Maggie You're bloody mad you are. Grow up Les . . . you can't have a kid, you're not even out of school. D'you hear me?

No response. Silence

Maggie What's his name then . . . your dad will want to know.

Lesley Orlando.

Maggie What sort of name is that. My God, he *is* black.

Lesley He ain't black. Even if he was it ain't none of your business now. I'm having this baby. I'm having it, and then I'm going. We don't need you.

Maggie Lesley . . . you must tell me . . . *is* he black, this . . . Fernando?

Lesley Orlando.

Maggie (*apologetically*) It's not me. It's your father.

Lesley Half-Spanish, he's half-Spanish.

Maggie (*relieved*) Oh. (*suddenly*) Not a bleedin' waiter is he? Typical. Bet he's Catholic as well. Better keep it from your dad for a bit.

86

Lesley (*leaving*) Least I told you.

Maggie You'd better be here when he gets home. How can I go to Bingo with this on me mind? (*turns up radio. Music. Closes her eyes*)

*

EXTRACT TWO

Lesley has a baby girl and calls her Chrissie. They move into a council flat. Lesley's Mum and Dad reject her and the baby. Orlando, the father of her child, decides to join the navy.

*

Lesley's flat. Enter Lesley with baby in her arms. She walks in silence around the room, listening. She rocks the child, gently whispering to her. Sounds of argument between a young couple who live upstairs. It increases in volume, disturbing the baby. Lesley tries to calm her down by telling a story.

Lesley When I was really little I wanted a toy pram. I wanted one so badly. I pestered Mum and Dad to give me one for Christmas. They couldn't afford it and told me not to be so selfish. But I couldn't stop. I cried because all the other girls on the estate had one. On Christmas Eve I went to bed thinking I weren't going to get one but secretly hoping still. I woke up at five the next morning and it was really dark. I couldn't see properly so I stuck out me hand to feel for me presents. I was rummaging around and touched something like a metal bar. (*grins*) I knew it. Inside I knew it. I switched on the light and there it was, a bright yellow pram. It weren't exactly what I wanted, but I didn't care. I was dead proud. And you know what? Found out later me dad had got it off the back of a lorry. What a joke.

87

She puts baby into pram. Sound of door knocking. Enter Isobel carrying sheets

Isobel It's taken me ages to find these, but never mind, not too late. Only been two days.

Lesley You bringing your washing round now?

Isobel No. You see this? (*holds up sheet*) This is the beginning of 'Trapping Jimmy'.

Lesley What are you going to do? Suffocate him with it?

Isobel I boil it up for three hours and then make him tea with the water. We'll have to have a party here or something.

Lesley Hang on . . . you're not going to cast any of your bleedin' spells in my flat.

Isobel It's not a spell, it's a charm. (*Isobel leaps about excitedly*)

Lesley Why would water from them sheets have any effect on Jimmy?

Isobel Because we . . . you know. He's definitely worth it, Les. Honest. Wouldn't bother if he weren't no good.

Lesley You reckon if you boil them sheets up . . . *then get him to drink . . .?!* I can't imagine Jimmy drinking a cup of tea at a party.

Isobel I've got to try. I'm a desperate woman.

Lesley Do you really think it will work?

Isobel Carla says her mum says her gran did it on her old man.

Lesley But did it work?

Isobel 'Course . . . well, I never actually asked her. But if this one don't, there are plenty of others.

Lesley Will it work on half-Spanish boys? . . .

Isobel (*interrupting*) Orlando? Didn't sound worth it to me.

Lesley . . . when he comes home on leave, maybe I'll give it a go . . .

Isobel We need a couple of pans. (*exits to bathroom*)

Lesley . . . does it keep fresh? If I do it now, I mean, he might not be back for a couple of months . . .

Isobel (*offstage*) You could leave them in soak, make it more intoxicating.

Lesley . . . I'll open the door, he'll have flowers in his arms, he'll pick us both up, Chrissie and me, twirl us round, give me a huge kiss. Then I'll make him a nice cup of tea.

Isobel re-enters carrying a baby's bath filled with water and begins to stir the sheets around

Lesley You can't boil 'em up in that.

Isobel No. I'll leave 'em in soak till tomorrow then I'll cut 'em up and stew 'em in one of your pans.

Lesley You ain't making a bleedin' casserole.

Isobel What we really need is one of them old-fashioned boiling tubs.

Lesley I think me mum's got one.

Isobel Can't you go and get it? Go on . . . please . . .

Lesley (*firmly*) No. I don't want to see her for a bit. Not for a long time.

Isobel But this is for a good cause.

Lesley I've nothing to say to her.

Isobel Well, get stirring then.

They both stir the potion

Lesley I feel right stupid.

Isobel Desperate women have to take desperate measures . . . (*stops*) . . . It's not going to work if you don't get into it.

Lesley I can't. I feel stupid.

Isobel Hubble, bubble, toil and trouble . . .

Lesley Leave it out.

Isobel . . .Hubble, bubble, toil and trouble . . .

Lesley Shuttup.

Isobel . . . Hubble, bubble.

Lesley Don't you know any other words? Hang on . . . eye of snail and something of frog. Never was good at English.

In the following sequence Isobel creates an atmosphere of intense concentration. Lesley tries, but remains self-conscious

Isobel Let's make one up. Come on . . . shut your eyes. (*they shut them*) Oooza Aaaza . . . Oooza Aaaza . . . (*Lesley giggles*) Zibba Zobba, Zibba Zobba, Jimmy wants his Isobel. Zibba Zobba, Oooza Aaaza . . .

Lesley Orlando wants Lesley as well.

Isobel What?!

Lesley (*feels Isobel's eyes on her. Opens eyes*) I'm getting into it . . . I'm getting into it.

Isobel (*shuts eyes*) Zibba Zobba . . . (*Lesley giggles again*)

Isobel (*pompously*) . . . Stop it. You are ruining my concentration.

Lesley I'm sorry Bel. I can't do it. I feel too stupid.

Isobel angrily picks up the bath and goes to leave

Lesley Where are you going with my bath?

Isobel I'm taking it home where I can concentrate.

Lesley What are people going to think with you carrying that around?

Isobel I don't give a stuff what they think. (*exits*)

Lesley (*shouts*) What am I supposed to wash Chrissie in?

Sound of door slamming. Lesley pauses, looks around the room distracted, then shuts her eyes tightly and holds out her hands as if to cast a spell

Lesley Listen to me Orlando
Listen to me sailor-boy
You fasten your shirt-buttons
Zip up good your trousers
You tighten your shoe-laces
Wash off your after-shave
But it won't work
Boy-in-blue
It won't work.

I've got your kid sailor-boy.
I've got your kid.

(END OF PLAY)

91

Ishtar Descends

by Nandita Ghose

Ishtar Descends *is based on an Assyrian myth which tells of Ishtar's descent into the underworld to search for her dead lover, and is linked here to the story of a modern day Ishtar; a young woman at a point of crisis. She, too, makes a journey into the 'Underworld'. In this last scene from the play, the ancient and modern worlds meet when Ishtar returns from a mental hospital.*

CAST

Erishkigel Goddess of the Underworld

Ishtar (*modern*) A young woman in her early twenties

Ishtar (*ancient*) The mythological Ishtar, same age as the modern day Ishtar

The Underworld. The Goddess, Erishkigel, addresses the bird-like mythological Ishtar who is silent except for the sound of a strange bird-like call. The modern Ishtar emerges from the shadows during the scene. She makes brushing movements as if to get rid of feathers that cling to her.

Erishkigel The dead kill the living. When he held you, he infected you with death. Your blood turned to fire and ice. You fell to the ground. You came looking for him and he killed you. Your new dress fits well. It clings on to you like a child's hand around a toy. Why do you try and brush it away? Don't you like it? Perhaps the colour is wrong? Or is it the length? Why don't you speak? I've given you food and drink and you've got nothing to say? Eat, drink — my little bird — why don't you sing?

Ancient Ishtar cries like a bird

Erishkigel Sing, sing.

The lights fade on Erishkigel. Modern Ishtar moves into a spotlight

Ishtar (*modern*) They let me out. I had a rest. A nice long rest. The medicine makes me sleep better at nights. I don't like it though. They make it taste sweet, but it's not. It's bitter. Makes you want to spit. I keep trying to spit out the taste, but it won't go. It's made me slow down. I can't do anything much. They calm me down. Calm and quiet . . . they nearly didn't let me go. I was so frightened they'd keep me in there. Every day, calm and quiet: 'Ishtar take your medicine. It's good for you.' They had me on a bit of string, pulling and pulling. They took everything, my freedom, my dignity, my liberty. Everyone in there was dead and I *knew* I'd died and was in hell. Someone gave me a little feather and I held it in my hand. It was the whole world to me, even though they'd given it to me to drive me mad. Am I mad?

Ancient Ishtar cries like a bird

Ishtar (*modern*) I'm all right Ishtar. It's all right. In the hospital there was a girl who never said anything. She cried all day and tried to pull off her clothes. She made these noises – strange – as if her tongue had been cut out. She was crying, but she sounded like a bird.

Ancient Ishtar makes sound like a bird's call

Ishtar (*modern*) She made these movements, trying to brush something away but it always came back. It clung on to her and she tried to brush it away but she couldn't get rid of it. Her hands were like claws. Sometimes she scratched her own face. She was somewhere where she couldn't get out. I wanted to help her but I knew she was dead.

Ancient Ishtar cries like a bird

Ishtar (*modern*) Every night I see her. She's lying in the dust under the ground. She's saying my name, over and over . . . Ishtar . . . Ishtar . . . (*pause*) I say to her, "I will find you. I'll hold you. I'll give you back your life." It'll be difficult, I know that, and dangerous, but somehow there will be a way in, and out again.

Ishtar (*ancient. In the voice of a bird*) Ishtar.

Ishtar turns and sees Ishtar. Fade to black

(END OF PLAY)

When Last I Did See You

by Lisselle Kayla

This play is about West Indian family life. Hidden in comedy it tells a story of Jamaicans lured to England on the promise of instant wealth in the late 1950s and early 1960s and describes the frequent destruction of family life, and the awareness that the rush to England was for illusory gold.

NOTES ON THE LANGUAGE OF THE PLAY FROM THE AUTHOR

In England today parents, young adults and children whose history is the Caribbean, see very little of their oral tradition in written form. For too long the Afro-European based languages of the Caribbean have been regarded as almost without value. Because of this, there still isn't a standardised dictionary widely accepted, but these languages definately do have a rich and colourful tradition, uniting and sustaining the self confidence of the peoples of these islands.

For more of these languages to be elevated to a position of pride, we must begin to play a part in the processes by recognising that they have a worth within themselves. In this play I have celebrated the language of Jamaica, showing it without compromise, as it has been fashioned by passing generations of people from the island. A glossary of terms and expressions is listed at the end.

CAST

Blossom Aged forty-five, a strong Jamaican woman with a good sense of humour. Lively and outgoing, with an inner strength not always appreciated by her children. Married to unemployed Fritz.

Miss Mary Aged fifty, Blossom's longtime friend from Jamaica. A Jehovah's Witness who has been dealt a raw deal in life by the god she worships.

Claudia Aged twenty-one, the eldest child who senses her mother's inner unhappiness. A serious and rather sedate young woman.

Shirley Aged seventeen, full of life and zest, the middle child still at school. Loud but likable, Shirley is closer to Lloydy than to her sister Claudia.

Lloydy Aged sixteen, the youngest, a teaser and a joker, he flits from one image and gimmick to another, with his dialect switching from broad Jamaican to pure Cockney.

EXTRACT ONE

A sprawling market of fruits and vegetables – mangoes, pawpaws, pineapples, star apples, sweet sop, sour sop, cho chos, pumpkins, green bananas, yams, cassavas, breadfruit – all piled high on make-shift tables, boxes, cartons, crates, baskets and mats. Amongst the appearance of colourful chaos town folk meander, haggling, bargaining and inspecting the produce with a critical eye.

Open to the steel band tune of 'Carry Me Ackee Go A Linstead Market'. A young woman dressed in Jamaican market fashion of the 1950s (colourful cotton frock with short sleeves and white calico apron, head tied with a gingham scarf) sits on the ground before a basket of okra. She is very pregnant, and harassed-looking, continually fanning herself with a kerchief against the heat of the midday sun.

Blossom   Okra, okra, six pence a pound okra. Come and buy you okra, six pence a pound. Nice and lovely okra. (*she talks to an imaginary customer*) Mam, hey mam – you want okra? Only six pence a pound. Look how it nice and fresh. When it cook it just slide down you t'roat nice and easy. Hey mam . . . hey! Yes . . . is you me talking to! Me not talking to you skirt tail[1] . . . Gwaan den![2] Golang![3] (*she shakes her head and talks aloud to herself*) Lawd, what a way dese people come in like hog![4] Dem waan come feel feel up and squeeze up, but not one ah dem waan buy me okra. (*pause*) Cho! What a life! (*sings mournfully to herself as she turns over the okras to protect them from the glare of the sun*)
Carry me okra go a Kingston Market,
Not a quati[5] would sell
Oh Lawd! Not a mite, not a bite
What a Saturday night!
Everybody come feel up, feel up,
Not a quati would . . .

A woman approaches, older in age, with a sackcloth full of wares balanced on her head. In her free hand she carries another sack

Mary Hello Blossom. Wha'p'n to business? It not so good today?

Blossom (*miserably*) Me no know one day when it good Miss Mary. Claudia jus' start school and me trying hard fe fin' likkle money fe buy her school books, but it look like de sun gwain dry up de likkle somet'ing before me can sell dem. And look how dem so pretty, ee.[6]

Mary (*sympathetically*) You must look after yourself and de pickney[7] inside you belly. If you don't careful it will nyam you out.[8]

Blossom But you must know how it hard Miss Mary. 'Specially when you have man who can't look after you.

Mary Fitzroy have hand and foot – him will find work.

Blossom Hand and foot? De man have good face and good voice – das all him have. How dat can feed me hungry belly?

Mary You can't put blame on him Blossom – him always try him best.

Blossom Me tired fe blame him. Is meself me ah blame now. Me married de man beca' him play one nice tune, sing inna me ears and dance two-step wid me. You ever hear anyt'ing go so?

Mary Why you haffe[10] run down de man so? You know him never have any money when you did married him.

Blossom Married? Hmmph! It never sweet[11] nobody

more than me when me did get married and tink me decent. If me did know marriage mean say you haffe carry unemploy' man pon you back plus him pickney – me would ah tek foot an' run long time!

Mary But you no know say it more hard fe man inna dis country? It hard fe we too, but at least we can always cook an' clean an' wash fe we likkle money. In town, man can't even find land fe dig.

Blossom But wha' me waan know is why me did haffe married if is only me can find work?

Mary You did do de right ting, Blossom. You did married in de sight ah God. Better time soon come, man. And when it come, you an' Mr Ricketts will know! So where him is now? Him still ah look fe work?

Blossom Him gaan ah Cuba, Miss Mary. Him use to did line up at de harbour, begging de people fe work wid de rest ah de man dem, and every day come back wid him two long hand. Me no know how him so damn bad-luckied. Is like me selling okra fe patch up him shoes leather . . . Lord Miss Mary, it look like de only way we husband can help we is to leave we.

Mary Have faith, Blossom. Times bad fe everybody. Everybody ah look fe dem likkle truppence . . . He', tek dis breadfruit and gi' it to Shirley and Claudia.

Blossom T'ank you Miss Mary, you is a real saviour . . . He', tek some ah de okra – enough deh. Me only gwain haffe carry it home wid me.

Mary (*putting some into her bag*) T'ank you Blossom, dese look nice and green and fresh. Me gwain miss all dese somet'ing when me leave dis ya country.

Blossom (*alarmed*) When you leaving? You papers come t'rough already?

Mary Yes, den me never did tell you? Herman get one job in de London Transport. It only leave only fe get ready. T'ank God fe Jesus!

Blossom Cooya![12] Is what you telling me! You mean say you soon run lef' me? Den is what gwain happen to you t'ree pickney?

Mary Lawd Blossom, it grieve me bad! All ah night time me can't sleep. We haffe leave dem beca' we don't have de money fe tek dem. We don't have not even a place fe stay when we reach Hingland. De Transport people give we job, but it look like dem no care 'bout how we gwain find place fe live. And me hear say it hard fe find room when you have pickney. Me hear say de English love dem pussy more than dem pickney. You remember Dotty who used to live near de gulley? She write her sister de other day. She tell her say how dem have holiday hotel fe dem pet! You ever hear anyt'ing so? Dem full up de daag wid so much food, it run it belly all over de place. So when you go fe step foot outta street, you fall inna daag do-do every time.

Blossom Dem glad fe know de daag dem so full up and can't run. You know how much time hungry daag inna Jamaica bite Fitzroy pon him foot?

Mary Well, whichever way it go, is not daag why we leaving go ah Hingland.

Blossom So how you gwain manage Miss Mary?

Mary Same way like how we manage inna dese hard time inna Jamaica. If me back broad enough fe carry Jamaica – it broad enough fe carry anyt'ing.

Blossom (*insistently*) But it no cold–cold[13] inna Hingland Miss Mary? Me hear say when you stand up ah street fe chat you business, you mout' just full up wid icicle. And dem have fog fe mek daytime come in like night time. Ah so me hear from Girlie man-friend inna Hingland.

Mary You can't spend you time listen to people ya. Me gwain find out fe meself. Anyhow, you see me? Me coming back quick-ah-clock. When me work de likkle money, is one big big house we gwain build inna Mandeville, so de pickney dem can have room fe play. Lawd, me gwain miss dem! But what fe do? . . . (*resignedly*) Anyhow, dem is old enough fe understand.

Blossom Den is who gwain look after dem? You can't trust any-and-anybody you know Miss Mary.

Mary Me dear sah! Me no waan nobody come inveigle me pickney dem. No sah! Me mother gwain tek Merna and Tanya, and me sister say she will tek Denzil. What a trial, ee! All dis upset and confusion just fe live life like decent people.

Blosoom Well at least Herman gwain have regular work now – and me hear say de money good in Hingland.

Mary It good yes, but you feget say is t'ree family me haffe support now?

Blossom But you no can work as well?

Mary Me tek all dat into account love. Blossom, why you don't send Fitzroy down ah de recruitment place when him come back? Dem still crying out fe people.

Blossom Him must leave Jamaica again, Miss Mary? And go all de way to Hingland? Is where we gwain find de money? Is struggle I struggle fe find minibus fare fe come ah market dis morning.

Mary De people dem will lend you.

Blossom Lend me? When me hear say is eighty pound one way fe one somebody, and is four somebody inna my family. Miss Mary, if me did have dat kind a money it would just help pay back what me owe everybody inna Jamaica.

Mary But you can't just give up so, Blossom.

Blossom Is not give up me give up, Miss Mary. Is fed up. No, Miss Mary. I not gwain trust any more money – otherwise is debt gwain bury me pon dis ya island. Anyhow, Fitzroy say him have him eye set pon America.

Mary Dem days gaan now, Blossom. You no see how America close up dem door pon we? Is only Hingland where dem want we. Unu[14] better hurry up mek up you mind before even dem close up on we.

Blossom Well, me wish you luck Miss Mary. It look like you chance come fe better youself. Me only wish de Fitzroy him coulda find work.

Mary Never mind Blossom, pray and de Lord God will hear you. Have faith Blossom, have faith . . .

Blossom Alright. Anyhow, tek care Miss Mary – me not gwain feget say is you did look after me when me did first come ah de market.

Mary An' tek care ah de pickney inside you belly.

Blossom Alright, mind how you go.

Mary T'ank you (*exit*)

Blossom (*wearily*) Okra, okra, lovely okra. Five pence a pound. Come and buy you lovely okra . . .

EXTRACT TWO

Years pass. Blossom, abandoned by her husband in Jamaica,

makes the journey to England where life is a continual struggle. She fights to buy her own home but misses the support of her family. Instead she maintains an uneasy relationship with Miss Mary and turns to a succession of boyfriends for support. Her children, Shirley, Claudia and Lloydy have grown up with only vague memories of their father.

FAMILY HOME, ENGLAND

Claudia is lounging on the sofa absorbed in a black women's magazine. Shirley is at the table surrounded by textbooks, trying to do her homework while rhythmically rocking to a Five Star track. Enter Lloydy with ghetto blaster, blasting

Claudia   Oh my God, not you as well! Turn that blasted thing off will you!

Shirley   Yeah! How am I supposed to do my work through all that!

Lloydy   (*not taking any notice*) Watch here Shirley, watch dis! (*demonstrates the latest reggae dance he has been practising in his room*)

Shirley   Turn it off, I'm trying to listen to my record.

Lloydy   Cho! You waan listen to some REAL music – dubstyle. (*turns up the volume. Shirley retaliates by turning up the player*)

Claudia (*sarcastically*) Why don't you two grow up! (*bell rings*) Turn it off! There's someone at the door!

They both oblige, and Lloydy opens the door to Miss Mary who is clasping a battered paraffin can and wearing a grim no-nonsense expression

Lloydy (*aside, and none too pleased*) Oh no, it's Miss Mary. (*then loudly and with forced cheerfulness*) Oh hello Miss Mary!

Mary What happening inside de house? What a way unu carry on when unu have white people fe you neighbour!

Lloydy Is music Miss Mary, music – and dem love it.

Mary Love what? How anybody coulda love dat deh bangarang?[15]

Lloydy But dem always bangin' on de wall when we stop Miss Mary.

Mary Stop you foolishness boy! (*entering room*) Dat same music gwain bring down de price of you mother house if you don't watch you step.

Lloydy I was just telling Shirley to watch de same ting Miss Mary!

Mary Where she is? . . . me not stopping.

Lloydy (*under his breath*) Oh good Miss Mary.

Mary What you say boy? . . . I was just on me way to buy some paraffin so I thought I would pass by and say howdy. Hello children.

Claudia Hello Miss Mary. Mum's not here. She's gone down the high street to buy a pair of shoes.

Mary Shoes again? But don't is only last month she buy a new-brand pair? Me can't understand how one somebody need so much shoes. Me done tell her already say she gwain wear out her foot-bottom before she wear out de amount of shoes she have.

Claudia Well, she'll be back soon. She went out about two hours ago.

Lloydy No she won't! She told me she was going out all day (*winking to Shirley*) – ennit Shirl?

Shirley (*conspiring*) Yeah! You know what she's like when she goes shopping for clothes.

Mary Well, I suppose I better not waste me time. Me haffe go back to work soon.

Lloydy Yeah, that's right Miss Mary, you don't want to waste your time.

Mary Me did only waan fe tell her say de church having convention on Saturday and I would come fe her if she interested.

Shirley Nah, that's not Mum's style, Miss Mary.

Mary Style? What you talking 'bout pickney? Me not talking boot and shoes – is Jesus Christ in Heaven me talking 'bout.

Lloydy Miss Mary, I tink Shirley mean say Mummy waan witness some more life before she give it to Jehovah Witness.

Claudia She's going to a club on Saturday anyway.

Mary Club? Den dem tings is not fe young people? What happen to Blossom? Why she can't rest her old bones now? Is about time she turn to God!

Lloydy Mummy say de best place to rest her bones is inside a satin coffin, Miss Mary, wid two Burlington catalogue on her chest.

Mary Is so she say? She no knew dat when she dead it will be too late? She need fe tek de hand of de Lord BEFORE him call her to de Judgement Gate.

Shirley Cor blimey Miss Mary! You sound like she's only got hours to live!

Lloydy (*mimicking and cupping both hands over his mouth*) Calling Blossom Ricketts! Calling Blossom Ricketts! Your time is up. You have two minutes to get to the Judgement Gate. Latecomers will be disqualified! . . .

Mary You gwaan boy! Is a serious ting dis. Not one ah we know when de good Lord gwain out de light. And beca' none ah we know, we must prepare long time before. Drop everyt'ing and follow de way of de Lord. You see you? You could be resting in you bed; you could be on de toilet seat; you could be putting up Christmas tree; you could be washing you foot; you could be buying two pound ah tripe; you could even be standing here strong-strong and talking to me when . . . (*she slams the paraffin can on the table. Bam!*) . . . de man out every blessed light inside you body. No man. You must always be ready. You see me? Me have me suitcase ready underneat' me bed full up wid new clothes.

Lloydy Why? Dem don't have clothes shop in Heaven Miss Mary?

Mary Me tell Herman long time. Me say 'Herman — when de Lord call me, I beg you do! Mek sure you dress me up while me still warm . . .

Shirley Urgh!

Mary . . . so dat when me spirit leave me, me know say me gaan lef' de world, decent in body as well as soul.

Claudia Gosh Miss Mary! You've got everything planned, haven't you?

Mary (*proudly*) You HAVE to plan these tings me dear.

Shirley But if you spend so much time planning for death . . .

Mary No. Not deat' my dear! Life. Dis is deat' what we living in now.

Shirley Yeah, alright then, if you spend so much time

planning for LIFE, do you have any extra time left to think about other things in life, I mean . . . (*looks confused*)

Lloydy   Yeah, like breathing for instance.

Claudia   Oh shut up Lloydy. He's only being silly. Have you always been a Christian, Miss Mary?

Mary   All me life dear.

Lloydy   I tink you mean 'all me deat', ennit Miss Mary?

Mary (*she glares at him before continuing*)   Me was born into de church, me grow up wid de church, and is de church leave to bury me now.

Claudia   What about Herman? Is he a Christian too?

Mary   But of course pickney! You tink me could waste me time wid any of dem fool-fool man outta de street? Me no like fe bad-mout' you mother, beca' me and she go back a long time, but all dem haul-and-pull-up[16] man friend she have – dem don't mean her any good. Me keep telling her. Me say 'Blossom, dem will drag you down! Dem will turn you into fool! Dem will mash you up![17] Dem will . . .' (*she suddenly becomes aware of her own excitement*) Cho! Me better hush me mout' before me run river inside de place. (*she notices Shirley's books*) Shirley. You doing you schoolwork child? Keep it up, de Lord know how you gwain need all de level you can get. What level you doing now?

Shirley   Well it's like this Miss Mary – I scraped through me 'O' levels, only just. And now I'm scraping through me 'A' levels, but I'm getting stuck at the 'O' level part of the course.

Mary (*impressed*)   'A' level and 'O' level! Yes, das what me did tink. Keep it up you hear girl? My big girl in Jamaica did do her exams and now she working in one ah de big-big bank in Orange Street. Every month she send letter, tell me how she getting on. Yes, keep up de good work child. If me and you mother did have de same edication you pickney have today, we would never be in dis country. And me would still be wid me t'ree pickney. (*sadly*) Ai sah! Life hard!

Claudia Don't you miss them, Miss Mary?

Mary Of course me miss dem. But what fe do? (*sigh. Pause*) . . . and Lloydy, what you doing wid youself boy?

Lloydy Not'ing much.

Mary Not'ing much? Boy don't stand here in front ah me and tell me say you doing 'not'ing much'. What you doing wid you under-ripe self[18] now you tek it pon yourself fe leave school?

Lloydy Mekking music Miss Mary – trying fe turn reggae superstar.

Mary (*kissing her teeth scornfully*) Mekking music me back foot! Why you can't go outta street fe find work boy? If you did stop talking wid de bad English and start comb you head and fling 'way de old frowsy hat, you would find job. Next time me come here me waan fe hear say you working. You hear me boy?

Lloydy (*saluting in mock respect*) Yes Miss Mary. Anyt'ing you say Miss Mary.

Mary (*casting an evil eye over him*) To tink is just de other day you was inside you mother belly and me was telling her fe tek care ah you! . . . (*turning her attentions to Claudia*) And Claudia, you still working in de people dem place?

Claudia Yes Miss Mary.

Mary Me can't understan' you young pickney. If you waan sing, why you can't sing inna de church instead ah dem fire-water place? You don't 'fraid you will turn drunk?

Claudia Miss Mary, I sell drinks and sometimes I sing. I don't lie behind the bar with a Vodka drip stuck in my arm!

Mary (*shaking her head with dismay*) Never mind. De good Lord will guide unu. Anyhow, me gaan. Mek sure you tell you mother say me did call. Is a long time now me don't see her.

(END OF PLAY)

GLOSSARY
[1]*Skirt tail* literal meaning 'I'm not talking to the hem of your skirt' but in this context it means 'don't turn away when I'm talking to you'
[2]*Gwaan den*! go on then
[3]*Golong*! go along
[4]*Lawd, what a way dese people come in like hog*! literal meaning 'how these people behave like pigs' but in this context is an expression of disapproval from Blossom about people not buying her okra
[5]*quati* literal meaning is a coin
[6]*ee* eh
[7]*pickney* child
[8]*nyam* eat *nyam you out* it will drain you
[9]*beca'* because
[10]*haffe* have to
[11]*sweet* pleases
[12]*Cooya*! an expression/sound
[13]*cold-cold* Jamaican dialogue often contains repetition of

words, for emphasis. Similarly see – strong-strong, fool-fool, big-big

[14] *unu* you

[15] *bangarang* noise

[16] *haul-and-pull-up* literal meaning 'dishevelled'

[17] *mash you up* destroy you

[18] *under-ripe self* immature

A Slice of Life

by Pauline Jacobs
and the Bemarro Theatre Group

A Slice of Life *was devised by five young black women from*
Second Wave and scripted by Pauline Jacobs. The original
script is a series of scenes linked by music, poetry and songs.
The play grew out of discussions and workshops around the
themes of friendship and choice. The group wanted to find a
way of portraying their lives on stage. These extracts are
flashbacks to the fifth year when the girls decide to leave school

CAST

Yvonne Fifteen years, dresses stylishly, acts older than
her years, hates school

Maxine Fifteen years, outspoken, honest and easy-
going

Julie Fifteen years, ambitious and determined

Pat Fifteen years, friendly, does not judge people
harshly

Miss Jones A teacher

Head The Head Teacher

EXTRACT ONE

A classroom. There is a low hum of chat in the background.

Maxine Guess what Pat.

Pat What?

Maxine Julie can't do her exam.

Pat What are you talking about?

Julie Miss said I can't do my Geography exam. I have to do Art.

Maxine Yeah. She ain't got no choice, man. That's wrong.

Pat Why won't they let you do it . . . have they said?

Julie Can you remember when I was off because Dad was sick . . .? Now they say I'm behind.

Maxine Ah true them don't know . . .

Julie I worked hard man, for my geography. Each sparing minute. Remember when you brought your homework to my house . . . going over it together?!

Maxine Stand up for your rights. I know, let's cause a riot.

Pat Don't be stupid Maxine . . . I've got it! When Miss comes in . . . let's all stay standing!

Maxine Yeah. That's a *good* idea.

Pat talks to the rest of the class

Pat Quick, stand up everybody! Miss won't let Julie do her exam.

Maxine Oi, stand up . . . stand up before I box you!

Miss walks in. Everyone goes quiet

Miss Okay girls. You don't have to stand for me.

Maxine We ain't.

Miss What was that Maxine?

Pat We ain't sitting down 'til you say Julie can do her exam.

Miss Whaat!! What's this you say girl?

Julie You know what, Miss. You and Miss Jones said . . . (*quietly*) I want to know why.

Miss We have discussed this before, haven't we?

Julie Look Miss, I want to see the Head. Art is not my choice. Why can't I do Geography?

Pat (*to Miss*) You just better go tek yourself and go find her . . .

Miss Patricia, leave the room. Go on – outside the door.

Pat leaves

Maxine Don't go Pat. Stay there . . . she can't do nothin' (*to Pat offstage*) Cho, you saff anyway.

Miss MAXINE COLBROOKE! – you can just follow your friend – OUT!

Maxine does not move. Stands defiantly

Miss Didn't you hear what I said? (*Miss grabs Maxine's arm*)

Maxine Don't you touch me . . . I can have you. I can have you for assault.

Miss Don't threaten me my girl.

Maxine And stop calling me 'your girl' . . . cos I

ain't. Don't let them twist up your head Julie . . .
stand your ground.

Maxine leaves kissing her teeth

Miss   Right, Juliet . . .

Julie (*interrupting firmly*)   Julie.

Miss   . . . maybe now we can talk sense, seeing as
your army has gone. I'm sure this little matter can be
sorted out easily . . .

Julie   This ain't no '*little matter*' to me, Miss!

Miss   . . . Just wait here. (*to the class*)   The rest of you
get on with your work.

*Miss exits. Maxine and Pat sneak back in and whisper to
Julie. Miss re-enters with Headmistress. Headmistress is
squinting and has a nervous twitch.*

Head   Now. What have I been called in here for?

Maxine   You mean to say Miss that you walked down
the corridor, up the stairs, down the corridor, up
more stairs . . . *and you still don't know what you come
up here for*!?

Head   I shall deal with *you* later . . . (*takes Julie to one
side*) Now Juliet.

Julle   Julie. *She* won't let me do my Geography exam.

Head   *You mean* Miss Jones. (*moves them both away*) Art
was your choice at the beginning of the term, so why
have you changed your mind?

Julie   No Miss . . . I didn't choose Art. You got me
mixed up with the other Julie. Julie Connell.

The Head now takes Miss Jones to one side. They whisper

Head   Can she tackle the exam?

Miss   Well, I'm not really her Geography teacher, but she did miss a few lessons when her father was ill.

Head   Can she cope?

Miss   Yes. I'm sure.

Head   Good. Otherwise we'll have a riot on our hands here . . . (*to Julie*) Okay Julie. But you must work hard and prove that you can do it.

Julie   It will come *naturally*.

Head   It just better had, my dear, it just better had.

Exit Head followed by Miss. Class cheers

EXTRACT TWO

Maxine and Julie are sitting in the playground. Tense atmosphere.

Pat   (*running on stage*) Julie! . . .

Yvonne comes on stage

Yvonne   What was old Miss Jones saying? She's saff anyway.

Julie   They changed their minds . . . I can do it!

Yvonne   Yeah. Gimme five . . .

They all slap hands

Yvonne   All right!

Maxine   Jus' 'cos they don't want no war . . .

Yvonne   When we get excited, feel good, talk loud . . . they think we're going to fight.

Maxine What about when we cuss, then? They must think we hate each other, guy!

They laugh

Maxine Is true. I can't wait to get out of here. What are you going to do Yve?

Yvonne stands tall, a little apart from the others. She is hardly in school uniform and is wearing make up

Yvonne ME! I'm taking the first slow boat to Jam-Down . . . *beeaautifuull* Jamaica.

Maxine Don't be stupid. What are you gong to DO?

Julie I'm not sure that I'm leaving yet . . .

Pat WHAT! . . . after today! You're joking ain't ya?

Yvonne What are you staying on for? . . . all of us is leaving.

Julie So what. We weren't all born together.

Yvonne Well, pardon me for breathing. You lot are well depressive, guy.

Julie I think I'll try a university!

All together (*loudly*) A university !!!

Pat That will be worse than here . . . all those people . . . nervous breakdown, man.

All together (*chanting loudly*) YOU WILL BROK DOWN.

Julie I knew you lot wouldn't understand.

Yvonne A slow boat to Jamaica sounds sweet to me . . . good sounds . . . subtle alcohol . . . meet a nice guy if you're lucky.

Maxine If you're lucky . . .

Yvonne *You lot would have to be*!

Pat What do you want Max?

Maxine I'm not sure . . . there's so much to do . . .

Yvonne Oh yeah. Tell me what.

Julie (*to Yvonne*) Just cool your mouth for a second.

Yvonne cuts her eye at Julie

Yvonne You t'ink se you is teacher now?

Maxine Maybe an artist. I can draw. You all *told* me I can draw.

Yvonne (*doing exaggerated motions of an artist*) Oh Monsieur, I would like to draw your outline . . . Ha ha!

Julie Why not!

Maxine But that means going to college . . .

Julie Don't let this place, or the people, hold you back. Too many black people get caught in that trap. I want to go further.

The others look at Julie

Pat My mum says that as you get older that gap's always there . . . there all the time. My mum reckons there's good and bad in everyone.

Yvonne Yeah?! Tell me about it. What does that say? Not everyone's black, has to play the fool . . . listen y'hear. I'm gonna do for *me*? (*kisses her teeth and looks at Julie*) She too follow fashion.

Julie What about you Pat?

Pat I don't know. All I know is, I ain't getting involved with no guy that uses me. (*looks at Yvonne*)

Maxine Too right. Not after the way life is so hard.

Yvonne You live life already? It ain't easy, you know.

Julie Well Yve, there's hope for you after all. You sound like an old wise-woman.

Yvonne Don't joke. It ain't funny.

Julie Ain't you got no sense of humour?

Pat Alright you two, keep it down.

Julie Well, it's her – she's too sour and stupid.

Yvonne And I suppose you're Jah's own personal lawyer . . .!

Julie Yeah.

Yvonne You've got an answer for everything

Julie Yeah!

Pat My mum reckons . . .

All together (*loudly*) OH, *YOUR* MUM!

Pat All the *good* men have gone in her generation.

Yvonne Then . . . where dem dey? Mek we go look fe dem now?

They all laugh as Yvonne leads off with a sexy walk

(END OF PLAY)

A Netful of Holes

Compiled and edited by Cathy Kilcoyne and Robyn Slovo

CAST

A group of teenage girls, school friends

Andrea Wise cracking, stylish and facety

Maureen The youngest

Jocelyn Andrea's side-kick. Nervous

Maggie Presents herself as a 'Good Girl'. Sensitive

Andrea's mum Working mother. Lives alone with her daughter

Ali Andrea's new older, and pushy, friend

Maggie's mum A strong, outspoken, no-nonsense, woman

TJ Independently minded, humourous

Angela Another teenager, same age

Beverly Another teenager, same age

Caroline Another teenager, same age

Mandy Another teenager, same age

A Netful of Holes was dev[...]
Second Wave *and performed at* [...]
in November 1984. It is a collection [...]
improvisation. As the title suggests, [...]
play without a main story, rather it is a [...]
descriptions and scenes created around the t[...]
leaving home. The style of devised work is [...]
and belongs to no single writer . . . these ex[...]
used to trigger ideas, develop the work further an[...]
discussion. Twenty two young women created [...] *play,*
drawn from their imagination and based on persona[...] *experi-*
ences.

EXTRACT ONE

IN SCHOOL
Andrea, Maureen and Jocelyn are in a school toilet. They
have max-pax cups of coffee and magazines, as the scene
opens they are settling themselves down with fags.

Andrea   Give me a light.

Maureen   Ssh. Keep it down.

Jocelyn   What you got next?

Maureen   Maths.

Jocelyn   French. She goes mad if I'm late. What's the
time?

Andrea   Ten past eleven.

Jocelyn   Got another ten minutes yet.

Andrea   Don't go Maths.

Maureen   I've got to.

Andrea   Stay here.

Maureen   Can't. It's a double lesson.

en   So. She'll miss me.

Andrea   Jocelyn?

Jocelyn   I've got to go.

Andrea   Boring.

Maureen   I don't fancy staying in here for a double lesson.

Andrea   It's very nice. Most comfortable loo in the whole building.

Jocelyn   It's like all the others.

Andrea   This is *our* toilet.

Maureen   They check the loos after break now.

Andrea   Go down the boiler room then.

Jocelyn (*interested*)   I've never been down there.

Maureen   I got caught the last time.

Maggie (*offstage*)   Can I come in?

Andrea   What for?

Maggie   A fag.

Maureen   We haven't got any.

Maggie   I can smell them.

Andrea   There's no room Pinnochio.

Maggie   Open the door.

Andrea   There's no room, there's six of us.

All start talking madly as though there are six of them

Maureen   Unless you stand in the bowl, there's no room at the inn.

Maggie   You in there Maureen?

Maureen   No.

Maggie   Quick, let me in. Someone'll come.

Maureen   Find your own toilet.

Maggie   Oh, let me in.

Andrea (*mimics*) 'Oh, let me in.'

Maureen   What's so special about this toilet?

Andrea (*interrupting*) It's *ours*.

Maureen   Who said?

Andrea   We did.

Jocelyn   I've got go French.

Maggie   No, she'll get in.

Andrea   Stay here.

Jocelyn   Let's all go then.

Andrea   Want to go down the boiler room then?

Maureen   Oh alright.

Andrea   You can come in now.

They open the door and all troop out. Maggie enters. They walk past

Andrea (*nastily*) It ain't the place and it's the people. Have fun. (*chucks her a magazine*)

EXTRACT TWO

ANDREA LEAVING HOME
Andrea arrives home as usual. Her mother is cooking the dinner

Andrea Evening Mum.

Mum Hallo. Go see to the meat. Had a good day?

Andrea Mum?

Mum Yes dear.

Andrea Can I talk to you?

Mum Are you working tomorrow?

Andrea I want to leave home.

Mum (*ignores this*) Don't let that meat burn.

Andrea Mum?

Mum What.

Andrea I'm thinking of leaving home.

Mum What!

Andrea I'm thinking of leaving home.

Mum WHAT!!!

Andrea I want to be independent.

Mum You are independent. You live your own life. I
don't trouble you when you come in, you go out. I
don't ask where you're coming from, where you're
going.

Andrea That's not what it is.

Mum I don't understand . . .

Andrea I'm moving out. I'm moving in with a friend.

Mum Moving? When?

Andrea Next couple of days.

Mum Next couple of days. What friend? So you can
go rub-a-dub and ting with that boy you met last
week? Is it so? No. You're not moving out. You stay

in that chair. You're eighteen years of age, you left school last month and you find yourself a job and now you want to leave?

Andrea I'm leaving.

Mum No.

Andrea You can't stop me.

Mum I can.

Andrea You can't stop me going out that door and not coming back.

Mum You been thinking about it?

Andrea Yes. I want to live my *own* life.

Mum You live your own life.

Andrea I want to make my own mistakes, to be a woman, a free woman.

Mum My God, what is she saying to me?

Andrea What you said round the table, about wanting to be free, when you were young. Remember? You were the same age as me, Mum, you can't have forgotten.

Mum No child. I've not forgotten. I haven't forgotten how hard it was, how painful. Andrea, that big blasted world doesn't care. *I care*!

Andrea I know Mum, I know all that. It's different now. I've gót a place, it's big enough for the two of us, I've got money and a job. You've taught me how to look after myself. I feel so good about this, excited . . . you've *got* to understand.

Mum There are some bad people out there. Bad, bad, bad.

Andrea Listen to me. I'm not going on to the streets.

Mum You're not going nowhere.

Andrea God, you make me mad.

Mum You're all I've got.

Andrea I've made up my mind.

Mum Why Good Lord? (*she breaks down*)

Andrea Shut up, Mum. Look. Don't cry. (*moves to touch her*)

Mum Get off me. Girl you have a lot to learn. I brought you up. I put clothes on your back and food in your belly. This is what I get. Stupid selfish child.

Andrea My bags are packed. I'm leaving the day after tomorrow. I'm going to live with Ali.

Mum Who's this Ali?

Andrea She's okay. She's older . . .

Mum It's not funny. You'll get nothing out of me once you leave.

Knock at the door

Mum Who's that?

Andrea It's her. We were going to show you the flat.

Mum Let her in . . . I got some things to say to her!

Andrea Mum I'm warning you, don't start.

Mum Let the girl in.

Andrea goes to the front door. Re-enter Andrea with Ali

Ali (*ignoring Mum, to Andrea*) Are you ready? My boyfriend's waiting in the car.

Mum What's your name . . . Alley cat?

Andrea (*to Mum*)   You make me sick you do.

Mum (*to Ali*)   So where is this place of yours?

Ali   Not far.

Mum (*to Andrea*)   If you think you're moving in with her . . .! (*to Ali*) You're not leaving with *my* daughter!

Ali   I'm not forcing her.

Mum   Who you think you are? Talking to me like that.

Andrea   Mum. If you don't stop, I'm walking out. (*to Ali*) Take no notice.

Ali   Do you want to see the flat, Mrs Martin?

Mum   I'm not going nowhere.

Andrea   Mum. Come on. Come with us.

Mum   No.

Ali   Come on. They're waiting.

Mum   They can wait. (*to Ali*) Now just get this straight . . . this is *my* daughter.

Andrea   Ten out of ten for observation.

Ali (*to Andrea*)   Shush. I understand how you feel Mrs Martin.

Mum   You? Understand how I feel? Have you children, child?

Ali   No.

Mum   Have you ever known what it was like to bring up a young child in a strange country? All on your own. No support, people attacking you on the street, calling you names, on your hands and knees cleaning up after filthy people, people that treat you like dirt.

Ali (*interrupting*)   You know I haven't Mrs Martin.

Mum   *I* have. And sometimes the only thing that kept me alive was my daughter.

Ali   Please Mrs Martin. Things are different now. (*pause*) Why don't you come see the place?

Mum   No. I'm tired. I'm staying at home. *My* home.

Ali   I'm going now. (*aside*) See you downstairs Andrea. (*leaves*)

Andrea   Mum. *Please* try to understand.

Mum   I'll try, but I don't think I will.

Andrea   For God's sake. It's only down the road.

Mum   It's not here.

EXTRACT THREE

Maggie comes home

Mum enters carrying the week's shopping. Maggie, her daughter, follows her into the house. Maggie is distressed and has been waiting outside the house

Mum   So you come back?

Mum (to audience)   Shim want me now. After shim up and come out me house. (*to Maggie*) You want independent then – so now you got it. What you want me for now? Answer me chile.

Silence

Mum   So where's Mikey? Hmm? (*she imitates her daughter to audience*) 'Mum, this is Mikey.' Mikey is a lazy good fe nothing. 'Mama, this is Mikey. Him and me want independence. Me want independence with Mikey.' Ha.

132

Maggie   Mum, please. I want to talk.

Mum   What you want? You want talk? Ha ha. Stubborn, stubborn, stubborn. You na want fe talk when Mikey standing here. Mikey. Huh. Stubborn. (*busies herself tidying up*) What you want? Money? I have none. (*to audience*) I know what she want. She want fe come home 'cos she pregnant. (*to Maggie*) Innit girl? You pregnant. You want fe know how Mummy knows? See dem breasts? Dem stand out two mile. She can't look me in the eye. Youse pregnant girl and now you want fe talk.

Maggie   Please, Mum.

Mum   No, no, no. You bring me trouble. Trouble girl. Always trouble. Is Mikey wit you now? (*no reply*) Is Mikey wit you now?

Maggie   He chuck me out. He say he don't want me.

Mum (*to Maggie*)   He say he no want you? (*to audience*) 'Mum this is Mikey', she say and come out me house. She can't cook or clean. She want 'independence'. (*to Maggie*) Independence turn round and say he saw he naw want you. So now you come home. You suck all the milk out me breasts and now you want more. Me saying no, you can't have no more, you took it all, you come out me house. No girl. No. You are not welcome. You hurt me. I don't want you in my house.

Maggie   Mum, calm down. Let's talk.

Mum   Sit down and talk. Talk all you want, I heard it before. Mikey talked. So what happened?

Maggie   I told Mikey.

Mum   Mikey. Ha, ha. (*to audience, mimics*) 'I love Mikey and Mikey love me.'

Maggie Last night. He was angry, he hit me and he say he want me to leave. He's different, he's changed.

Mum Mikey, he got what he wanted and now he don't want you.

Maggie I'm frightened. I don't know what fe do . . . tell me what to do.

Mum You left here like a big woman and you come back snivel like a child. He won't take responsibility. You have to take his responsibility on *your* shoulders, and let me tell you someting – you need big, strong shoulders for that and you no have it.

Maggie But I want to keep the child.

Mum See where your stubborness gets you child? I could have told you, helped you, but no. 'I love Mikey and Mikey love me', and you had ears for nothing I had to say. Now you want fe know what fe do. I told you – independence is hard, you have to fight for it. You don't lay on your back and get it – that's na freedom chile. You heard none of it and all I can say now girl, is the ball's in your court and right now me na feel like playing tennis.

EXTRACT FOUR

HOSTEL SCENE

Angela, Maggie and TJ are lounging in front of the TV. The living room is full of magazines, clothes, coffee cups and so on. Maggie sits eating huge chunks of cheese out of the packet

Angela Give me some of your cheese.

Maggie Buy your own.

Angela Give me some.

Angela goes to grab the cheese. Maggie pulls away

Maggie   Get off.

TJ   Right you two. I want to watch this TV programme tonight. Eight o'clock. Got it? Eight o'clock. I'm telling you.

Angela   She's telling us.

TJ   So you know.

Maggie   What if we don't want to watch it?

TJ   I don't often want to watch things. Just tonight, okay.

Angela   I bet it's some boring documentary.

TJ   No. So don't turn it over or nothing, or else. Give me some of your cheese.

Maggie   For God's sake.

TJ   We should operate the telly room 'democratically'. (*they all look at each other*) You know, take votes on what to watch. Then there's no argument.

Angela   Wonderful. Come here everybody. Listen to this smashing idea that TJ's just had.

TJ   Don't be funny.

Angela   She's leaving soon and she's coming out with all these ideas.

TJ   Jealous?

Angela   Of you? No darling, never.

TJ   Jealous of my new flat.

Angela   I'll have one soon anyway. Yours is in a crummy area.

TJ   It's a start.

135

Maggie   You've waited long enough.

Angela   Have you seen it?

TJ   Not yet. It's quite small, one bedroom. I'm going to paint it white and olive green.

Beverley enters in a dressing gown. Her hair wrapped in a towel

Beverly   Who left a piece of paper in the bath?

Maggie   Caroline, she likes writing.

Beverly   That's what I love . . . bathing with sheets of foolscap.

Maggie   Did you read it?

Beverly   It was a bit difficult. When I found it, it was stuck to my thigh. It was wet and all the ink had run.

TJ   The best thing will be living without other people's dirty knickers all over the floor and washing dripping down your back when you're in the bath.

Maggie   It said: 'Clean the bath'

Beverly   Oh.

Maggie   Well, did you?

Beverly   What?

Maggie   Clean the bath.

No reply

Beverly   (*calling to offstage*)   Caroline? Come here a minute.

Maggie   When are you leaving TJ?

TJ   When I get the keys, week after next.

Beverly Lucky thing. Get out of this dump. Honestly I'm sick of this place. I swear I'm getting out of here.

Angela Yeah. I know. So are we all. Moving out tomorrow to a semi-detached in the suburbs.

TJ This will be the first time in four years where I'll be on my own, not crammed up with other people, just on my own. Not having to worry about where to sleep at night, or having enough money to go from one dole office to the other. Not having to live with 'mad' people. (*makes mad face*)

Angela Thanks. (*laughs*)

TJ This place is like a half-way house you know. You've got somewhere to live but it's not a home.

Beverly (*shouting*) Caroline.

Angela Anything's better than the streets.

Caroline enters

Caroline What do you want? I was washing my hair.

Beverly You left a note in the bath.

Caroline Yes. It said 'Please clean the bath'.

Beverly Well, it's in bits all *over* the bath. You put it there, you clean it up.

Caroline You're so petty. You better not have used all the hot water. (*leaves*)

Beverly And someone – *Angela* – used my shampoo.

Angela Don't look at me.

Beverly Let me smell. (*smells Angela's hair*)

Angela I've got my own.

Beverly I put a line on it and someone used it. You

have to keep everything locked-up in this place . . . no-one's got any respect.

Angela Once upon a time in a fridge in a house lived six bottles of milk. Two were called Beverly. One called Maggie, one called Caroline and two called TJ. They live happily together and they all *stink*.

Maggie I've said it before. We should share the milk.

TJ Some people do more sharing than others.

Mandy enters holding jar of coffee

Mandy I just sat on this . . .

Doorbell rings

Maggie I'll get it.

Mandy I found this jar of coffee under a cushion in the sitting room.

Beverly So no-one can find it.

Beverly tries to grab the jar and they struggle

Angela You're so selfish.

Mandy No. No. *I* found it . . . *I* want a cup of coffee. (*grabs jar. Runs offstage to the kitchen*)

Beverly (*shouting*) Buy your own.

Mandy (*shouting back*) Finders keepers.

Beverly I put it there so no-one would use it.

Angela Quick. In the kitchen . . .

Angela, TJ, Caroline exit for the kitchen, laughing

Mandy (*offstage*)   Want a cup of coffee?

Beverly   Ha ha!

Mandy enters

Mandy   Do you always hide things in odd places?

Beverly   Have to. Gets used otherwise. You'll catch on. DON'T offer your fags. DON'T let people use your stuff. DON'T lend clothes. Otherwise, you'll muck yourself up.

Mandy   No chance of that.

Beverly   Too smart eh? I've heard that one before.

Mandy   Well, you know. Everyone seems so nice here.

Beverly   Better than a lot of places.

Mandy   There's a good atmosphere.

Beverley   How long you been here?

Mandy   Few days.

Beverly   You'll learn. (*exits*)

(END OF PLAY)

No Place Like Home

by Roselia John Baptiste

This play examines the word 'home', the country where one was born, the members of your family, the place where one likes to be, the place of origin. For Black Britons, those who were born or who have lived in Britain for a number of years, the word is difficult to define.

CAST

Maggie (*Mother*) Dominican, mid-fifties. Dwells on her past and drinks whisky to help her forget

Thomas (*Father*) Dominican, mid-fifties. Charming

Marcie (*Daughter*) Eldest girl, twenty-two years. Left home to live with her boyfriend. Close to her mother. Seven months pregnant

Anne (*Daughter*) Youngest, eighteen years, preoccupied with her studies and 'getting on'. Close to her father

Jimmy & Coozi Middle-aged, West Indian. Thomas's fairweather friends

EXTRACT ONE

MARCIE COMES HOME

The living room. Marcie puts on a slow lovers rock, sits down, hugging her belly. Enter Maggie. Pause. They look at each other. Neither moves

Marcie Don't start Mam.

Maggie I don't say nothing. (*pause*) The suitcase I see in de passage is yours?

Marcie Yes.

Maggie You down for de week-end ne?

Marcie No, I'm back home.

Maggie You back home. Bon Dieu Seigneur Mari Josef . . . Oh Marcie, Marcie, Marcie. You turn big woman now, chil' turn dat blasted music down.

Marcie turns the record player off

Maggie You see all your friend having chil' so you want chil' too en it? I suffer you know, I suffer to bring all you children into dis world and all you fardar don't do nothing . . . You and Trevor getting married? Why all you cannot save all you money? Buy a house? Married wid nice clothes? Why all you cannot do me proud? I suffer, all you don't know how I suffer. Up to now all you have a sister back home, because I didn't have money to send for her. Now she big woman, she can look after herself. When I come to England expecting you, I had to work in a hospital, a big hospital in Lewisham. I had to raise you in one room, you and Annie. And your fardar. Your fardar go meet his woman . . . leave me in de house, me alone . . . wid two kid, expecting

Wendell. All you don't know . . . all you don't know. (*pauses*) Marcie I want you to have more.

Marcie Anne says you've been drinking a lot.

Maggie Anne don't know nothing . . . (*turning away*) right, let me go do my cooking . . .

Marcie Mam, you always turn away from me. Why won't you let me know you and try and understand?

Maggie I have to go cook for when Thomas finish work.

Marcie You've never once talked to me, never told me anything apart from how you've suffered. Why do you tell me if you don't want me to ask questions. You like to talk but you don't like to listen.

Maggie Marcie, I send you to school to do better than me. When Etta send me to school, I never go. But you, you can read and write – you should know better. You have an education in England.

Marcie Education in England! You think because I can read and write I have no problems. I'm black. I'm still your daughter with or without an education. I'm still your daughter . . . but all the time you shut me out.

Maggie gets up

Marcie You try to make me English. You think I have nothing to learn from you. You think if you talk you might contaminate me. That I wouldn't be English enough. But I'm not English Mam, and I'm not Dominican either. *Why won't you talk to me*?!

Anne (*off-stage*) I'm home. What's for tea Mam?

Maggie (*relieved at interruption*) My Cooking! I have to go do my cooking . . .

Exits to kitchen. Anne enters

Anne I SAID . . . what's for tea? (*then pauses, noticing tense atmosphere. Marcie exits pushing past Anne angrily*)

Maggie (*now off-stage*) Deh have some soup in de kitchen. I know you don't like lamb, so I boil soup for you.

Anne Thanks. (*hangs up her coat, takes a book from her satchel and sits down. Maggie re-enters, sits and watches the television intensely*)

Anne (*looking at her mother*) I can smell whisky . . .

Maggie Is it? Just a little drop I drink this afternoon, you can smell it? You see, all of you, you and your fardar is the same you know, a little drop of whisky I drink since afternoon when I come home from work and all you think I drunk, in it?

Anne sighs deeply

Maggie Yes I mad in it?

Anne I didn't say anything . . .

Maggie You think I didn't hear you, what you say. What you say?

Anne exits to kitchen

Maggie Yes. Just go leave me alone, all of you is de same. Leave me here alone, in it? I going to my bed anyway.

Lights fade

EXTRACT TWO

Two months later. The Christening. Enter Thomas with

cigarette in his mouth, his hat pushed up untidily

Thomas I'a Grandaddy! I'a Grandaddy . . . me,
Thomas Joseph Reuben Williams is a Grandaddy. (*he
sings and dances*)
Erica Why ay ay
Erica why ay ay
Erica why you like to push your bumbum outside
put your bumbum inside . . .

Thomas (*turns towards door, shouting to his friends*) All
you not coming inside den eh eh? Come get drink
man! Come and wet de baby head.

*Enter Coozi and Jimmy, Coozi carrying a box of dominoes,
Jimmy carrying a pack of beer*

Coozi (*giving dominoes to Thomas*) Well, empty de
bones ne man!

Thomas Gi me a chance . . . gi me a chance.

Jimmy (*holding bottle of beer*) How you 'spect we can
open dis wid no opener?

Thomas Des one in de kitchen.

Jimmy So you not going to help ya guest den?

Thomas You cannot see I doing something eh eh.
(*Thomas shuffles the dominoes. Jimmy goes into the
kitchen, Coozi and Thomas pick up their dominoes*)

Thomas (*to Jimmy*) Come if you playing ne man.

Jimmy I coming, I coming.

Thomas (*laying down the domino loudly*) Sixes. (*they
play*)

Jimmy So where de baby is den?

Thomas Which baby?

Jimmy Which baby? You call us to wet de baby head . . . now you axin which baby?

Thomas De baby sleeping man. Wha you axin me for baby for? You go sof' ne or wha?

Enter Anne with tray of drinks

Coozi Is Annie dat ne? But look a child dat grow pretty . . . come let me see you.

Thomas Annie all right you know, one of the best daughter any man could have, and she love her daddy you know. Come give your daddy a kiss.

Anne Dad . . .

Thomas What ne? You think you too old to give your daddy a kiss . . .

Anne goes over to her father reluctantly and kisses him on the cheek. The men all laugh. Anne exits embarrassed

Thomas Her and Marcie make me proud, not like that mal'prop boy I have in my house, coming and going when he want. It's his mother's fault you know . . . His mother that make him turn de way he is . . . the boy spoil . . .

Coozi All de children nowadays is so they is. I have one, make de wife cook him food wid no meat, tie up him hair like a plant growing from he brain, and when me eating pork chop now he have de bloody cheek to call *me* nasty.

Jimmy Finish wid children now man and lay down de double tree.

Coozi puts down the double three. Jimmy slaps down a domino

Jimmy Three one. (*he laughs*) All you wasting me time talking about children. This is serious money business.

Thomas Okay. Serious business now . . . (*he wins and rubs his hands together*) real serious business now.

They start a fresh game

Coozi So Annie not courting then? She don't have boyfriend?

Thomas What you mean. She only a child we . . . She only eighteen you know and you asking if she have boyfriend? Four and three. I am telling you when dat little girl of mine bring a boyfriend home, I know he will be de right one for her. Dat girl is like her mother – she know how to choose de boys.

Maggie/Mother (*off-stage*) Thomas. Thomas . . .

Thomas Sacre Tunere, every time I playing a little game she always have to call me. (*sweetly*) Yes, what you want?

Maggie You and who there?

Thomas Me alone . . .

Maggie You talking to yourself den?

The men laugh. Enter Maggie

Maggie Look how Thomas scratching my table, Bon Dieu . . . Eh Coozi, Jimmy, you there den? How about de wife Coozi, the foot any better.

Coozi Martha alright . . . sometimes de foot does

bodder her. The cold gets to de old bones now . . . 's all the clothes she used to wash in de river start to play on de old bones now . . .

Thomas   Look come all you, lets talk about old times. Where's Annie? Where's Marcie? Annie, (*shouts*) Annie, Marcie. Come. We going talk . . .

Enter Anne, followed by Marcie

Thomas   Come children, come sit down. Let me tell you things you don't know about life. You kids born here don't know a 'patat' about life. Come everybody, let's talk old times. Let me tell you about love . . .

Maggie puts on a loud calypso tune and begins to dance

Thomas (*shouting*)   All you think when you have chil' all you in love? I'm telling you when I did fall in love wid your modder I did know it was *real* love.

Thomas tries to dance with Maggie, she exits to the kitchen, Thomas turns down the music

Thomas   Yes, me an your modder is real love . . . (*Anne laughs*) What you talking about you laughing? When I was nearly your age I fall down in love wid your modder.

Anne   How is it I'm not old enough to have a boyfriend then?

Thomas   Oh dat's different . . . I was a man. Anyway back to all you modder, I used to see dat woman walking through de Savana every day, and you see your mam? She was a real lady. She never want anybody to do anything for her. If she want

149

anything, she get it herself. But I liking this woman so much, I want to do something for her to notice me, anyway one day I see her coming through de Savana carrying some basket of fruit home for her modder . . . and I see her dere . . . a real strong woman you know . . . and I go up to her, and I say, real nice I say: 'You want me to carry dem mango for you lady?' The woman just give me one kind of look, up to now I don't forget it, she make 'stuups' and she just tell me to move from her way. But I just pester, pester de lady until she say 'I do' . . . Was 'I do' ne or 'I will'? Can't remember, but we never regret it, en it Maggie?

Maggie does not answer

Thomas All your modder . . . she's the best woman in de world I telling you . . . and all you think you in love? Now let me tell you about love.

Enter Maggie

Maggie What you know about love Thomas? You know anything? You don't tell dem de same time you used to watch me in de road you already have three children with three women in Roseau? You don't tell dem when you come to England how you run leave me don't tell me nothing. How it was my brodder that have to pay my passage to come find you? You tell dem how when you reach London you take two woman again and leave me in de house wid three kid . . . you tell dem dat eh eh. Den don't bodder tell dem nothing about love because you don't know a patat . . . (*picks up a bottle of whisky. Exits*)

Coozi (*embarrassed*) Well, I tink it's time I was going to see what de wife cook for me.

Jimmy   You going Coozi? I coming. See you, you hear Tom . . . Okay . . . (*Coozi and Jimmy exit*)

Thomas   What I say ne?

Annie (*pours Thomas a drink*)   Tell us one of your stories Dad.

Thomas   You like to hear a story en it my Annie . . . You like to hear your old dad talk, but sometime he does talk a little too much . . . (*drinks. Laughs*) Eh eh when I was young I was a real nice looking man you know, if you did see me wid my nice clothes on Sunday, well tack down. I used to go to church and I could sing, could sing like an angel, me. I was in de choir, and at dat time it was an honour to be in de choir you know . . . (*he drinks*) At dat time children were children, I would never cheek my father like all you talk to me. No sir . . . (*laughs, remembering*) I remember one time I didn't listen to what my modder and farder tell me. All you know. Soo koo yeh?

Anne and Marcie shake their heads

Thomas   All you don't know Jee weh? witch ne? Diable? Devil? Well back home everybody believe in spirit, but me being young I decide not to listen to what my modder and my fardar tell me. I had to go to a place and to reach it I had to pass through a wood. My modder tell me if I see a donkey I must pull down my pant, pull out one of de hair from me backside and kiss it, to ahm . . . get rid of de evil spirit, you understand? Anyway it was dark, dark, dark, but me being a man I decide to pass through de wood and forget what my modder and fardar say. I was walking along den I hear a little sound behind me, I just carry on walking, but I still hearing de sound. 'Clip Clop, Clip Clop . . .' I looking behind but I still walking, you understand? I don't want to appear foolish . . . but all in me mind I hearing me modder and me fardar saying 'Thomas drop your pant, Thomas drop your pant'. I start walking fast. I running. I reach a big tree in de middle of de wood and I rest by de tree. Again I hearing 'Clip Clop, Clip Clop', de sound was getting louder and louder, closer and closer. I don't know if it was Jee weh, Diable, I don't know what it was, I just drop me trousers and take off. Up to now I don't know what de hell it was behind me. I never look back . . . is true . . . (laughs)

Enter Maggie

Maggie All you want supper?

Anne Yes please.

Thomas If you making.

Maggie exits to the kitchen. Thomas looks at his glass with nostalgia

Anne Don't you ever feel like going back?

Thomas All de time girl, but a man has to go forward, no sense looking back . . . Your modder now, she is living in de past, mess up your mind to keep on looking back on things.

Anne Could drive you to drinking?

Thomas Your modder is all right you know girl, she's a good woman. I'm talking serious now, she's de best . . . just nowadays I just can't . . . can't seem to . . . to talk to her.

Marcie Why don't you go home Dad? Take mum home. We big enough now to take care of ourselves.

Wendell finish school this year . . .

Thomas When I win de pools . . .

Marcie You don't have to win the pools to go home. Take early retirement, you have a little money saved up and uncle won't let you starve.

Thomas You make it sound so easy.

Anne It is, if you put your mind to it.

Thomas You think Maggie would come?

Marcie Ask her. Mum (*shouts*) do you need any help?

Exits to the kitchen

Thomas (*to Anne*) You know your modder. (*pause*) The place must have changed, it not home any more, in a sense I'm more English than Dominican. I've been here for more years than I was over there. And you don't see me buy me British Citizenship last year? What kind of welcome you think they'll give somebody who sell his birth mark?

Anne Thatcher could have thrown you out any time.

Thomas Well maybe it is better she do dat instead of me paying good money to be British.

Anne Why are you making excuses? I thought you wanted to go home.

Thomas Home? You don't understand Annie. My Dominica is in my head, yours is in your heart . . . and your mammy's . . . (*looks at the bottle of whisky*) How do you see Dominica, Annie? How do you picture it? You never see it . . . all you hearing is story, story, story . . . Tell me what you see . . .

Anne I see palm trees and sand . . . the bluest sea and the bluest sky . . . hot sun and a cool breeze . . . I dream of Dominica sometimes. I see black people, some real black with pearl white teeth and grass skirts, I know it's not like that but that's what I see . . . and straw huts . . . I see straw huts . . .

Thomas   You see through white man's eyes

Anne   I didn't ask to be born here. (*pours herself a glass of whisky, then pushes it aside*) I know from what Mam has told me, there are wooden verandahs and I can see Grannie sitting there in her rocking chair smoking her pipe. And Uncle Jerome with his gold teeth and his shop and Uncle Nicko with his red face drinking his white rum and . . . and . . .

Thomas   They are ghosts, Annie. Those are things from bygone days . . . they're dead.

Anne   (*ignoring him*)   And I see a young man chasing a young girl and loving his youth.

Thomas   He dead too.

Anne   Dad, you're fifty years old, you still have half your life to live.

Thomas   So what you think is over there for me now?

Anne   Your brothers . . . your mama's grave . . . home.

Thomas   Is true. That *is* home, mama. You understand? Is where you come out, from inside your mama belly, and baby when you come out there ain't no going back. Home is my mama and my mama is dead.

Maggie and Marcie enter, laughing, from the kitchen with a tray of food

Maggie   Mangez. Mangez. Eat. Eat. Where's de music. Faces too long in here . . . de party don't finish yet. *(puts on a calypso record and pulls her husband to dance with her. Thomas and Maggie dance together)*

(END OF PLAY)

Fallen

by Polly Teale
Researched and developed with Carole Pluckrose

This play is the result of a four month collaboration between actor, writer and director and was inspired by news coverage of what became known as 'The Kerry Babies' Case' following the discovery of two dead babies in Ireland in 1985.

Set in rural Ireland, Fallen is fiction. It is not an accurate account of any real events, or persons.

CAST

All the characters are played by one actor – Siobhan

Siobhan Yeats Young Irish Catholic countrywoman. Grows during the course of the play from childhood to her mid twenties. Disarmingly honest, bold yet private

Prosecution Voices from Siobhan's trial – the Prosecutor, Doctor and Prosecution witnesses

Tobias O'Rourke Siobhan's lover. A married man, older than Siobhan

Anne O'Rourke Tobias' wife. A woman in her late twenties

Auntie Maudie Siobhan's elderly aunt

Colleen Siobhan's elder sister

Fallen was originally performed in 1986/7 with Arc
  Theatre
Directed by Julia Bardsley
Acted by Carole Pluckrose

Fallen *fluctuates between adult reflection and action playing out the current moment. It is a monologue, played by just one actor. Individual characters can be defined by changes in voice and posture or by turning back to the audience. Siobhan dresses and undresses at various times during the play. Sometimes she wears a dress, jumper and coat, at other times only a slip.*

Music playing an old Irish folk song. As the audience enters Siobhan Yeats is standing motionless centre stage amidst a wreckage of upturned chairs and scattered objects. A carving knife. String. A bucket. A white sheet and discarded pillow. All are used during the course of the play.
  Suspended mid-stage is a sash window. Beside it a table and chair. As the music plays out, Siobhan looks about her. During the following tape recorded voice-over she clears the stage, returning each object to its place, and folding the sheet carefully away.
  Tape recorded voice-over begins. Voices of the prosecutor and prosecution witnesses.

Prosecutor Did you love Siobhan Yeats?

Tobias I suppose I did.

Prosecutor Is that your answer?

Tobias I did, yes.

Prosecutor How much did you love her?

Tobias Depends on how you mean 'love'. I was a married man.

Prosecutor Did you ever intend to leave your wife for Siobhan Yeats?

Tobias No.

Prosecutor Was she a virgin when you met her?

Tobias No.

Prosecutor May I ask, who was it suggested you pull your car into a side road on that first drive home?

Tobias Maybe she did.

Prosecutor So, Siobhan Yeats had a previous sexual history. She has sex with a man who offers her a lift home from work. Is it not then possible that she is mother of both babies, the one found on the farm and the baby found stabbed on the beach? Is it not possible that she was impregnated by two different men within the space of twenty-four hours resulting in the differing blood groups of the two infants. (*pause*) Tobias, your evidence is that you think it was *she* suggested you stop the car that first night?

Tobias It's possible.

Different voices from the Prosecution

– Did she love this man, or just what this or any other man was prepared to do with her?
    – She displays callousness and an incapacity for love and attachment.
    – I manipulated her breasts to see if they were lactating.
    – No sense of shame or apparent regret.
    – A liar and manipulator, a trait particularly prevalent in attractive women.
    – You really believed he would marry you? Like a prince finding his princess and putting her up on his white charger.
    – Exhibit 49B, Siobhan Yeats, soiled panties.
    – What kind of a lady are we dealing with?
    – I put it to you that the reason you did not go to hospital, the reason you did not tell your friends, was that you had no intention of letting that child be alive in this world after it left your body?

Siobhan kneels at the table, she is wrapping something in newspaper. She talks to herself with the voice of a child

Siobhan Me and Colleen seen the cows 'doing it'! When they put their thingies out long, we have a competition see who dare touch it. She's rubbish. We seen them doing it loads of times. Our black cow had a baby. I held its legs and pulled it out with my da It's all covered in blood and keeps getting stuck halfway. I'm not scared of blood though, I like it. I get it all over me hands like my da. He says if you get blood on your hands you can say you've got 'bloody hands'. (*giggles*) We eat our animals. I seen me da kill our piggy, he's called Porky, but he's glad we killed him because he's tired and worn out. Porky screamed even when he's dead and there's blood pouring out. (*pause*) I won't eat the porky meat, I keep thinking one of the bits might be his thingummy. Me da says I've got to eat it or he'll lock me in my room till I do. So in the end I put it down me pants and pretend I ate it, then I wrapped it up and buried it in the field. Next day me mam tell me all the porky meat's been sent away, and it's only ordinary meat now from the butcher's.

Sings 'Here comes the Bride' as she buries the parcel in the field. Kneels down and crosses herself. Says the 'Hail Mary'. It gets faster and faster

Blessed art thou amongst women . . . amongst women. A monk swimming. Blessed art thou a monk swimming. (*she giggles*) You say a word loads and loads of times and it comes out like rubbish, like a cow mooing. Siobhan Yeats. (*she repeats it until it becomes nonsense then says it slowly.*) Siobhan Yeats. (*she writes in an exercise book.*) Siobhan Moriarty. If I married Paddy I'd be Siobhan O'Riley. Can't have that, my 'r's are awful. (*looks out at the audience*) He's out there somewhere and he doesn't know I'm here and I don't know where he is. If I married someone with the same name I wouldn't have to change. Siobhan Yeats.

Sits back, covering her face with the exercise book. After a few moments she is shaking with laughter

We done the reproductive system in biology. Locusts, frogs and humans. We took them down off the board, then two minutes before the Angelus, Sister Jocelyn asks if there's any questions. As if anybody's going to say any of them words in front of the whole class. (*pause*) Next week she gave us 'the' talk. She says, we're not to sit on boys knees or run in the street. She keeps saying men are weaker than women. Weaker? She says women must protect them from their weaknesses. No matter what a man says he won't respect a girl if she lets him. (*pause*) Clare Donovan's sat all the way through with a big smile on her face, like she knows it all. *She'd* be smiling if she knew what they call her at the boys' school! (*pause*) 'No-one's going to want soiled goods,' that's the only thing me da ever said about sex.

Siobhan gets up slowly taking a pillow from a chair at the side of the stage

He got ill when I was fifteen. I went to see him at the hospital. He was lay there all wired up with a mask on his mouth like them films at the end when the heart beat thing's going smaller. I hate hospitals, don't trust them. You could have cancer, they'd tell you it's a toothache. (*pause*) Next week coming home from school I seen that all our cows were still out in the field, so I knew. (*pause*) They're all stood in the kitchen waiting for me. (*starts to laugh*). Colleen's thinking I'm not understanding. She's all red and crying and tries to put her head on my shoulder.

The pillow slips to the floor. She lets out a cry and falls to her knees. Sobbing, she beats the pillow as if having a fight and shouts at the audience

There's people coming around saying how sorry they are about me da. I don't believe they're sorry at all. What are they sorry for? (*pause*) Me mam keeps on crying all the time. Me da never cried, not even when he was dying. She gets right on my nerves. I shout at her. She doesn't understand. (*stands hugging the pillow to her*) Me da was clever. He knew about things. He's the only one ever really understood me. (*pillow is returned to the chair*) There's his shoes still in the cupboard.

Music, the soundtrack of a film. Siobhan sets up three seats as if in a cinema. Lights dim

February the thirteenth, nineteen seventy eight. I'm asked out by Tommy Hooley from Hooley's farm. He's twenty-three years old, been out with loads of girls from school. Susie lent me her new dress on condition I tell him it's hers. He's wearing the same old usual things. Good job I took some money because he never offered to pay for the cinema. After a bit he leans over, puts my hand on his trousers. (*pause*) I can feel it through the material. I'm embarrassed in case anyone can see but then he puts his coat over both our laps. He's undone his zip. Starts moving my hand up and down. I make out like I've done it loads of times but it feels funny. My arm's killing me. He's watching the film as if there's nothing happening! (*The film soundtrack reaches its*

crescendo and fades. Lights up) I got no tissues so I wipe
my hand under the seat. When the light comes up I
don't want to look at him. (*she imitates him*)
– Aren't you going to give your boyfriend a good-
    night kiss?
– You're not my boyfriend.
– You do that for anybody do you?
– I do not. Bloody cheek.
Then he kissed me. It was lovely, really gentle. Says he
wants to see me again.

As she talks she moves the 'cinema seats' away

So that's how it happened. The third time we went
out. I'm thinking about soiled goods. If I ask him to
stop halfway through am I saved or have I already gone?
It's too late. I've done it. I didn't think it would be like
that. I kept thinking something would happen. (*pause*)
We're not a lucky family when it comes to men. My
mam's the only one in four got wed. One of my auntie's
a nun. Married to God. The other's a priest's house-
keeper. All them years washing his socks and cooking
his meals and not so much as a kiss. (*pause*) Auntie
Maudie who lives with us was asked to be married loads
of times. She kept saying 'no'. She says 'there's nothing
a man wants more than what he can't have'! (*pause*) She
never got married in the end. Our Colleen's thirty, I
don't think she's ever been kissed by a man.

Pause. Looks to the audience with sudden excitement

I seen this great job advertised at the sports centre in
Tralee. They just built the whole complex. All brand
new. The latest thing. You could eat off the floor. The
girls there dress up like it's Saturday night every day of
the week. I wore my new blouse for the interview, but I
felt like a right old tramp. I never thought I'd get the

job. The first week I never said a word. Kept thinking Tommy Hooley might turn up to meet me. He's getting real serious. Says he loves me. There's this bloke at work. One of the groundsmen. They call him Tobias O'Rourke. He keeps knocking on the window, pulling faces at me when I'm working. S'a nice name isn't it? Tobias. Like a name from a story.

Stands with a drink as though at the counter in a cafe

One day I'm in Bewleys and Tobias O'Rourke comes in with *her*. He's touching her all the time. Whispering. Laughing at every word she says. Holding her hand under the table. He's real nice looking. Then she gets up to go to the toilet and I swear. She is ugly, fat nearly, and he's looking at her like she's the rose of Tralee. He's looking at her like there's no one else on earth. How could he have married her? When she's in the toilet he smiles at me (*smiles back*) He smiles at me all the time now, comes up and leans on me, calls me his private leaning post . . . bloody cheek! (*pause*) He sent me a card for my birthday. (*gets it out of her pocket*) It's got a dog on the front of it, says 'Be nice to me, I've had a ruff day'. Ruff spelt R–U–F–F, love Tobias, cross cross cross. (*as if talking to Tobias*) Tobias, could you drop me off at the bus stop?

Sound of windscreen wipers. Lights dim. They are in the car

S'a nice car. (*to audience*) Says he'll take me all the way. Says they got the Abbeydorney bus timetable in the library under local myths and legends. (*laughs to Tobias*) I'm learning to drive. (*pause*) Don't be daft, we'd crash. (*pause*) No. (*pause*) You keep your hands on the wheel? (*pause*) You promise? (*she leans over and puts her hands on the wheel. He accelerates*) Slow down. I'll kill you . . . Tobias, slow down for God's sake. (*she falls forward as car stops suddenly, covering her face with her hands, miming. He takes her hand away, we hear her intake of breath. She kisses Tobias. She is shaking)*

Soft instrumental music, a haunting melody. It is the middle of the night, she lies on the floor, head on the pillow

Sometimes I feel like there's two men inside of him. One that I love and the other . . . like if I catch his eye when we pass in the town. I don't know how he can pretend like that, as if he never set eyes on me, and only the night before we were making love in the car. He's the devil. He's crazy for me, looking at me like he'll go mad and fall out of his skin. He's wanting and wanting. Me, feeling like I'm made out of glass and I'll break if he touch me. (*she sings 'Lord of all Hopefulness'*) Baby Jesus I'm singing a hymn. (*gets up*) I wonder is he's awake? Five miles. Two hours to walk. Three quarters on a bicycle. A minute if I fly.

Gets up opens the window and leans out. She shouts

Tobias! Tobias! I love you. I love you. I love, love, love you. (*she laughs helplessly. Closes the window*) It's autumn, I hate the autumn. The leaves so beautiful. After, it's always like I missed it. Just when I think it's there I look out of the window and they've fallen. (*pause*) He brought me a gold cross and chain for Christmas. I told him he shouldn't be wasting his money on me. How's he going to explain that to his wife? (*as if talking to Tobias*) What's she like? (*pause*) I mean as a person? (*pause*) I hate knitting, it's boring. (*pause*) How d'you meet her? (*pause*) and? (*pause*) Just wanted to know. (*pause*) Typical man. Tell you the time and place and think that's the whole story.

Turns her back, so becoming Tobias' wife

166

(*sharply*) Siobhan Yeats. I think you know who I am. I'm not after apologies or explanations. Just stop what you're doing. Just say you'll stop and leave us alone. D'you hear me? D'you hear what I'm asking you?

She turns, reassuming Siobhan

Everyone's pretending to be working. I get up to go to the toilet, leaving her in reception. There's a bulge under her coat. She's expecting a baby. I'm stood inside the toilet and I hear her come in and wait outside. I flush the chain and open the door. She's stood right in front of me. (*as if responding to Mrs O'Rourke*) Is it my fault he's not happy in his marriage? (*slaps her own face. Pause*) How dare she? How dare she come into where I work, telling me to get my claws out. Some people have got no pride. Why does she not tell *him*, her own husband? Because she knows why. If he loved her, why would he be wanting me? (*sits back at her desk*) After, everyone's asking me what I've done to my face. (*in reply*) It's a rash. Must be the soap. (*to the audience*) She had the baby. It was early, a boy. Toby's away from work, two weeks without a word.

Places a salt cellar on the table. It is the work cafeteria. She sees Tobias coming over and looks away

Oh, so you decided to come and sit with me have you. (*pause*) Don't expect me to talk to you. I don't talk to strange men. (*pause*) I'm not your servant. Get it yourself.

She moves the salt away then snatches it as he tries to pick it up

Ask nicely. Say 'please', say 'Siobhan you are

fantastic and I am stupid, thoughtless, selfish'. (*pause*)
Go on say it.

*She takes the salt from behind her back and pours it into into
his tea*

'I am stupid, thoughtless and selfish.' (*pause*) Oh, did
you not want it in your tea?

*He grabs her arm, pulling it up behind her. She breaks free
and turns on him with the salt pot like a knife*

Don't you . . . don't you dare touch me! (*she watches
him leave . . . and lets the salt cellar drop*) I'm wanting and
wanting him, but as soon as we're together I start an
argument. I cry while we're making love. (*she sits*) Make
out like he's hurting me. Then after I won't let him
come near. As soon as he's gone I'm sorry.

Pause. She looks up suddenly as though asked a question

We were driving back one night when this car
overtook us and Toby says 'It's my wife'. I thought he
was kidding because we got this joke that she's always
around the corner like the bogeyman. Then the car in
front slowed down. Next thing I knew, she was
opening the door on my side, got hold of my arm. She
was shouting, calling me 'whore', 'tart', 'slag', 'prostitute'. Every insult under the sun. Pushing me from
behind. I thought she was going to kill me.

As if to Tobias

'Go back to your wife Tobias. Go back to your wife.'
I gave him a choice. He didn't have to choose me but he
did. *That* night he chose me. We walked cross country
to his friend's house in Spar. All the way we neither of

us said a word. We'd sometimes be holding hands, then he'd help me over the wall, open a gate for me. It's twelve miles we walked, but I don't remember. I felt sort of light, like I didn't have to move my legs to keep walking. We could go on and on and never come to anywhere or ever see anyone. We're together. Now she'll have to accept that we're in love. She's the fool not me.

(*unbuttons her blouse*) I am carrying his child.

(*she takes off her shoes one at a time. Looks at Tobias.*) We slept in the same bed that night. We took all our clothes off. I never seen him like that before. All over. I never seen any man. It wasn't like I expected. He looks more like a child. I want to curl him up like my little baby and put him to sleep in my arms. (*she throws her shoes to the ground, livid*) Next day half of Kerry had heard what's happened. Mrs Moore walked past me in the street, not a word! She can talk. When her Sheelagh got married she had a bouquet the size of a bush. It's born three weeks after the wedding. They're hypocrites the lot of them. I had to tell my mum about the baby. I thought she'd go crazy, but she just cried.

Her voice unsteady . . . as if to Tobias

. . . Tobias! (*pause*) I think, I don't know. But my period. It's late. (*to audience with relief*) He just kissed me so I knew everything was going to be all right. (*picks up a sheet and begins making a bed on the floor*) He says if there's an emergency I'm to call him at home. He won't be able to speak, but I can talk to him. If it's an emergency I can just pick up a telephone and he's there any time I want. I don't feel so much as if I'm leaving him as I did before. Part of him's still with me. (*she feels the baby kicking*) Is this enough for an emergency? I could just tell him and put the phone down. He doesn't have to speak. (*smiles*) No. I'll wait. Tell him properly. I want to see his face.

Gets into bed she has made. She is in hospital after the birth of the baby

Annette's born. May 30th at three in the afternoon. Five pounds three ounces. I told Theresa to tell him. That's at half past four. There's visitors six till eight. I'm tired. It's sore, bruised, bleeding like a tap. So I ask the nurse for a mirror. Try and make myself half decent. If he walked in now he'd probably walk straight out the other door. She's very friendly, the nurse. She says 'It's always the first request. Make up for damage done.' She said, 'We had a lady last week. Ninety-two years old and died with her lipstick on. Lay there, pale as a turkey's neck with two pink lips. What a way to meet her maker.'

Pauses

Me mam, Colleen, our Shane, Padraigh's all sat round the bed taking turns to hold Annette. Everyone says she's beautiful. I wonder might he come later on. If he couldn't get away he might come later. Will they let him in though? Will they let him come in after visitors? Would he say he's the father. It's his child. It's his baby. (*pause*) The next day Toby came, five minutes before the end of visitors.

As if to Tobias

Hello

She recounts their conversation

– You alright then. Everything go alright?

– You want to see her?
– It's a girl?

– Didn't Theresa tell you. I told her to tell you.
– Ah, she must have, I forgot.

– You want to hold her?
– Not just yet. Don't want to do any more damage.

– You hold her.
– The nurse said not to disturb it.

– *Her*, Annette. You're the father.
– Shshsh, now I got to be off. I bought these. (*she is given imaginary flowers*)

– You going?
– You get better eh!

– I am better.
– You get back to normal.

– You got to go?
– Goodnight now.

She calls after him

– See you then.

(*angrily*) They're trying to make me breastfeed her. I don't want to. I've had the baby. I've done it I'm not a cow, I'm a human being. (*pause*) He didn't come again. It's hard for him, coming to the hospital. I understand his position. If he's going to leave her there's no point causing more pain than necessary. She's no need to know about the baby.

Back at home. She stands, the baby is crying

All right! All right, I'm coming. Okay. I've heard you. Shut up! I said shut it! Shut your face or I'll shut it for you. What do you want? What the hell do you want? (*screams into the baby's cot*) What do you want, what the hell do you want? (*pause*) Shut up!

Sudden change of mood. She is getting ready to go out, pulling on clothes as she talks

They put Toby on late lunch so I don't see him at work. (*to the baby*) Shshsh, Mammy'll be with you. (*to the audience*) 'She's' causing trouble again. Gets suspicious if the petrol's down. He gets away for half an hour or so. (*calls to her sister*) Colleen, Annette's crying. (*goes to the baby*)

Colleen! Annette needs changing! I'm going out, won't be late. (*drops the clothes she is holding and pushes the objects from the table to the floor. Sits astride the table*)

When we make love I think of him with her. I think about him touching her. Putting his fingers inside her skirt. Down her blouse. Undoing the buttons, to her bra. Her breasts. Him kissing her breasts. Sucking them. (*she buttons up her blouse quickly. As if to Tobias*) Don't go. Stay and talk. (*pause*) Do you love me? (*pause*) Do you? (*pause*) I love you.

(*to audience*) Sometimes he looks at me like he doesn't know who I am, like I'm rubbish. Dribbling down the seat . . . leftover. (*she closes her legs, adjusting her skirt*) Theresa gave me some contraceptives. She gets them through the post from a cousin of hers in England. I never seen one close up. It's disgusting. I'm not using that! why should I? I love him. Why should I put that between us. Spoil it? What would he think of me all prepared like the regular little expert? There's names for girls like that (*proudly*) I couldn't stop him if I tried. If you saw how he looks at me just before we make love. He's like a wild animal. He'd rip the world apart if I made him wait. That's when I know. You can't lie with your body. I know I'm the only one in the world and he hates her for thinking I'm a whore, because he loves me.

She returns home. She pulls the rocking chair into the room as she speaks

My auntie Maudie's up when I get in. She's sat with a drink and the radio on, as giggly as a girl. Tries to make me dance with her round the kitchen. (*in reply to Maudie*) I'm no good at dancing.

She sits in the rocking chair, back to the audience. She becomes Maudie. She lights a cigarette

Nonsense. If you can walk and you can count you can dance! You should enjoy yourself while you're young Siobhan. Don't listen to any of 'em. Dried up old prunes, 'pray to the blessed Virgin'! And do you know why? They never done it an they're damned if you're going to get away with it. Jealous little bitches. Pray to the blessed Virgin! You don't fool me love! They're well known them Hebrew milkmen! (*laughs*) We're fallen the minute we're born. The Devil's got us by the ankles so where's the point pretending to be angels? We'll all be sorry in the end. I don't like the daytime Siobhan, I've seen it all my life and I'm sick of it (*she points towards the window*) Look out there. Now there's pretty for you. Fairy lights. We could be anywhere, any time forever and ever amen. It's all the same at the end of the day. It'll be just the same when I'm not here to see it. Just exactly the same.

Turns to the audience as Siobhan

Poor old Maudie. She's gone right off the rails. She was found once in the cowshed. No clothes on, stood there, singing to the cows, naked as the day she was born. I don't mind it when she's like that really, trying to make me dance round the kitchen. It's worse when she's sat quiet. Sat watching the dot on the television since closedown, like it's a programme and she's waiting for it to end. (*pause*) Should have got my curse fifteen days ago. I wake up in the night, look on my finger for the stain in the dark. Takes ages to see properly. (*she crosses herself*) I've been late before. It doesn't have to mean that.

Music, old traditional folk song. Siobhan is wrapping a parcel

I got the afternoon off work. It's our Christmas party tonight at the Meadowlands hotel. The shops look beautiful. I wanted to buy something for Tobias. It's always difficult to buy for a man. They never seem to know what they want, not like a woman. (*she looks at the jumper*) Forty inch chest. Pure new lambswool, keep him warm. It's expensive, but it's worth it to get something special. Something to last, that he can wear. He doesn't like jewellery. (*pause*) I bought the others from work a large 'Quality Street' to share. I'd spent too much on the jumper. (*she finishes wrapping the parcel*) There. I love wrapping them up. I love a parcel. A mystery. (*writes the tag*) Tobias. Love Siobhan. Cross, cross, cross. Could be anything.

Christmas party music. She walks forward with the parcel and 'sees' Theresa

It's for Toby, a jumper. Cost forty-five pounds. (*pause*) I don't know. He'll say it's a present (*pause*) I don't know do I? (*her smiles fades, as she sees Tobias and Mrs O'Rourke through the window*) How dare he! . . .

174

how dare he! Tell him I want to speak to him. (*she runs out*)

Sound of pouring rain. She lifts a sopping wet jumper out of a trough at the back of the stage and holds it over her head. She is soaked. Shouts through the rain at Tobias

Toby, is it true your wife's pregnant? (*pause*) So am I. (*pause*) Am I sure? (*sarcastic*) Is she sure or is she just pretending? (*pause. Repeating him*) 'Come down to Earth'! Tobias I'm having another baby! (*pause*) Leave her. Come away with me. We'll go somewhere. Start again. Get away.

Starts talking to herself

He won't let me go, surely to God he won't let me go. He'll come after. He'll follow me to the ends of the earth because he loves me. (*shouts after him*) TOBIAS! (*silence. Sound of rain*)

I could see them all dancing. Doing a conga. Holding each other round the waist. I wanted to go back inside. I wanted to go back inside. I want to go back inside.

Soft instrumental music. At home in her bedroom. She pulls strips of paper off the sopping parcel. Pulls off her sodden clothes and crawls into bed . . . but is restless and after a few moments awakes. Puts her hand down to her stomach, remembering the baby

(*whispers*) Damn you. Damn you. (*goes to the window and looks out*)

I wish I was a cow in the dark, in a field, and nobody took any notice. Who cares which is the father or what you did to get like that. You just are (*she looks at her hand on the glass*) If I push my hand against the glass it'll break. There'll be blood everywhere. It'll all be over. If I push my hand . . . (*she falls to her knees*) Hail Mary full of grace the Lord is with thee. Blessed art thou amongst women and blessed is the fruit of thy womb, Jesus. Holy Mary, Mother of God, pray for us sinners now and at the hour of our death Amen. Oh God!, oh God! I promise I'll never go with anyone again. Dear Mother of God. I'll go to church every morning. To confession every day. I promise I'll never go with anyone ever ever ever. (*she wakes Annette*) Annette? There there . . . shshsh. (*she gathers her in the sheet*) Everything's going to be all right. Shshsh. Mammy's going to have a baby. You're going to have a little brother or sister. If it's a girl we'll call her Noreen. If it's a boy we'll call him Shane. Maybe tomorrow we'll tell Theresa. No, we'll not tell anyone. They'd never forgive us a second time. (*pause*) I found some of me Da's old jeans in a drawer. They look all right with a jumper pulled over, no one would know. (*clasps her stomach in sudden pain. A contraction*) Oh God! It can't be. It's too soon.

She turns becoming Colleen, Siobhan's sister

I knew Siobhan was pregnant. She fell over in the field when we were cutting the turf and her jumper came right up. I was ashamed in case our Padraigh seen it, but he never said nothing. We just both laughed because she fell over. She knew I'd seen it. She gave me a look. She's real quiet all the time now. She sits looking out of the window like she's waiting for someone. You can't say nothing to our Siobhan. You can't say nothing.

Pauses. She reflects

Before I went to bed I'd made a hot chocolate.

Siobhan was out the back door so I asked her if she wanted one but she was feeling sick. I had seen some blood on the kitchen floor so I wiped it up and went to bed. I was praying to the statue of Our Lady on the mantelpiece. She was glowing in the dark. Looked like she was floating. My Auntie Bernie brought her back from Ballinspittle where she seen the statue move. She got right up close on account of being a nun. She bought the luminous one to keep away the evil spirits and bad souls in the night. I could see her on the mantelpiece and I was praying for Siobhan and the baby she was carrying. Even though she never told us, we all knew. You can't hide that. We seen the bulge, we all seen it . . . (*she is interrupted by a recorded scream outside. Runs to the window and shouts*) Siobhan! Siobhan!

She turns and becomes Siobhan again

I'm all right. I'll be in in a minute. (*walks backwards, colliding with the bucket. Washes between her legs, then takes the babys' body and wraps it in a fertilizer bag. She talks to herself*) I had a miscarriage. A miscarriage. God carried him away. I had a miscarriage. (*carries the bag forward looking for a hiding place. Thrusts it beneath a chair. Finally she goes back to sit at the table*) Oh my God! Oh my God!

She remains behind the table. She is now at the police station under interrogation. A bright light shines into her face

I told you I had a miscarriage. (*pause*) I had a mis . . . (*pause*) Can I go home now? (*pause*) Can I go home? (*pause*) Heard about it. (*pause*) Read about it in the paper. (*pause*) A baby found stabbed on the beach at Cahiraveen. (*pause*) Must have been a mad woman to kill her own baby.

She realises they think it is her

I had a miscarriage. (*quiet. Averts her eyes*) All right, I did have a baby, but it's not the same one. I had it in our field. I was on my own. I pulled it out with my own hands. It never breathed nor cried nor nothing . . . I buried it in the well behind our barn. It's still there, in a plastic bag. (*pause*) Looks like a piece of rubbish, but it's my baby. (*pause*) What? (*pause*) No. (*pause*) I mean, I don't know. (*pause*) I don't remember. It was dark. (*pause*) Please. (*as if a piece of paper has been put in front of her*) What's this?

She reads. Hesitant, and with disbelief

I picked up the bathbrush and the carving knife with the brown timber handle that have been shown here today. (*puts paper down and listens to tape recording*) I went back to the bedroom and hit the baby over the head with the bathbrush. I had to kill him because of the shame it would bring on my family and because Tobias O'Rourke would not run away and live with me. The baby cried when I hit it and I stabbed it. (*pause*) It stopped crying. There was blood everywhere on the bed and also blood on the floor. I threw the knife on the floor. I told them I would have to get rid of the baby. Everyone was panicking. The boys put the baby in a plastic bag similar to one I have been shown today. The boys left in our car. I changed the sheets and took my baby Annette into bed with me. About five fifteen, I got up and took the brown bucket with the afterbirth in it and put the afterbirth in the old hay by the well. Then I washed the knife and the brush and put them back in their proper places. When the body of the baby was found on the beach at Cahiraveen I knew deep down it was my baby. I was going to call him Shane. I am awful sorry for what happened. May God forgive me.

She whispers the last few lines with the tape and then looks (*slowly*) So what you're saying is . . . If I sign this statement I can go home?

Silence. She pulls herself up from the table and moves towards the chairs

The Ban Guarda says they're taking me to a psychiatric hospital. She brought me some books to read, 'True romance' series. I started one but I couldn't get into it. (*pause*) I'm not at all well. There's a television at the end of the ward, but the sound's turned down so I'm reading the news for the deaf. (*pause*) They've found my baby in the well. The baby found stabbed on the beach has the wrong blood group for me and Tobias (*pause*) We don't have to go on trial. They've dropped the murder charges. Thank God. (*pause*) We never did nothing. They *made* us make them false confessions.

Sets up the chairs as if in a court room

They locked us away in different rooms for hours and hours. They were bawling and shouting. They said 'They've all confessed it, Siobhan. The whole family. 'Tis only you won't admit what you've done.' There were noises in the next room. It was our Padraigh. Sounded like a fight. I could hear Colleen crying. They showed me the statement our Padraigh signed saying he and Colleen hid the baby in the boot of the car and drove in the night, thirty-five miles to Slea Head, where they threw the baby out into the sea. (*pause*) In the end I would have said anything to get out of there. I wanted to go home. I wanted to see Annette. (*pause*) 'She'll be took away,' they said. (*pause*) 'We'll put your mam in a mental home and the rest of you in jail', he said. (*pause*) 'tis unknown how many you've killed between you and buried out there in the field. That poor baby, that poor innocent baby. His face will haunt you for the rest of your life.' (*she sits*)

Our lawyers say the police'll be sweating now. Half of Ireland's waiting for an explanation. They're setting up a special tribunal to investigate Gardai behaviour. Now justice will be seen to be done. Now everyone'll know what really happened. (*pause*) There's people from the newspapers coming to the hospital. They want to talk to me. Take photos. I look a right mess. I'm on the front of the Irish Times. Colleen says I'm famous. (*pause*) I hope they're not too hard on Tobias at the tribunal.

She turns to face the witness box as if looking at Tobias. The text of the tribunal as heard on tape at the beginning is now repeated by Siobhan with disbelief

Did you love Siobhan Yeats? (*pause*) I suppose I did. (*pause*) Is that your answer? (*pause*) I did, yes. (*pause*) How much did you love her? (*pause*) Depends on how you mean 'love'. I was a married man. (*pause*) Did you ever intend to leave your wife for Siobhan Yeats (*pause*) No. (*pause*) Was she a virgin when you met her? (*pause*) No. (*pause*) May I ask, who was it suggested you pull your car into a side road on that first drive home? (*pause*) Maybe she did. (*pause*) So Siobhan Yeats had a previous sexual history. She has sex with a man who offers her a lift home from work. (*pause*) Is it not then possible she is mother of both babies? The one found on the farm *and* the baby found stabbed on the beach. Is it not possible she was impregnated by two different men within the space of twenty-four hours resulting in the different blood groups of the two infants? (*pause*) Tobias, your evidence is that you think it was she suggested you stop the car that first night. (*pause*) It's possible.

As she repeats the following lines she takes the chairs one by one and throws them to the ground. Her voice is becoming gradually more angry

Did she love this man or just what this or any other man was prepared to do with her? (*pause*) She displays callousness and an incapacity for love and attachment. (*pause*) I manipulated her breasts to see if they were lactating. (*pause*) No sense of shame or apparent regret. (*pause*) A liar and manipulator. A trait particularly prevalent amongst attractive women. (*pause*) You really believed he would marry you, like a prince finding his princess and putting her up on his white charger. (*pause*) Exhibit 49B, Siobhan Yeats, soiled panties. (*pause*) What kind of a lady are we dealing with? (*pause*) I put it to you that the reason you did not go to the hospital, the reason you did not tell your friends, was that you had no intention of letting that child be alive in this world after it left your body?

She breaks down

I didn't kill my baby!

Screams, runs to the window and is sick. Closes the window. Clears away the debris of litter and chairs. Gradually the stage is as it was at the beginning. She talks as she walks

Tomorrow, I kept thinking I'll do something about it tomorrow. I felt so ashamed. It's different the second time. We all make mistakes, but twice. That's not daft, that's bad. (*pause*) I got what I deserved didn't I? (*pause*) Sometimes though, when I remember what happened to us at the station, I get so angry. I start sweating all over like I'm ready for a fight. I have to walk till I calm down. You can walk a hundred miles though. You can fly round the world and it still comes with you. (*pause*)

You can jump off a cliff and it still comes with you. I seen them pictures in the paper. Her with her arms wrapped round him all smiles. They don't fool me. He never loved her and he never will do. He's just married to her that's all.

I don't suppose anyone will want to marry me now. I think I'm an unlucky person, never won a raffle in my life. They say though that God gives to them that can cope, the greatest load. He's given me good things too, like Annette, and the twice out of three times I've seen the Kerrymen play at Munster Park they won the final. I never brought them any bad luck. (*pause*) And when me and Colleen went to Ballinspittle we saw Her move. I thought, after everything . . . you know . . . but we both saw Her, waving and swaying like, and Colleen said she was looking specially at me and I thought so too.

Music. Irish folk song, same as in opening scene. Lights dim slowly

(END OF PLAY)

Biographical notes

Roselia John Baptiste was born in Bradford in 1962, the eighth of nine children of Dominican parentage: 'The name Roselia John Baptiste came from by grand mother's name Roselia La Guerre, and my mother's maiden name Agnes John Baptiste. I never met my grandmother but I believe her strength and spirit are within me and I know the determination and perseverence of my mother is in my blood. I dedicate my writing to them both. I wish to thank my family for their support as always: my father for his stories; my brothers and sisters for their "gossip"; my nephews and nieces for their listening ears in hope that they too might "pass the word"; and I would also like to thank Devon for his patience.'

The Bemarro Theatre Group are young women from Second Wave who set up their own performing group. They aim to show positive and entertaining material for young people in and around South-East London. Established since 1986, following the successful tour of *A Slice of Life*, the Bemarros tour a workshop programme and devise their own material.

Briony Binnie was born and brought up in Bradford, Leeds. Her first play, *Tom, Dick and Harriot*, written when she was twelve, won an award at The Royal Court Young Writers Festival. *Foreshore* is her second play, written when she was fifteen, and was produced by Second Wave as part of the Second Wave Festival 1986. Briony has written a new play for an all-female cast, set in a girls' school.

Ann Considine is the Co-ordinator of Second Wave and organiser of the Second Wave Festival of Young Women Playwrights. She directed *Foreshore* for the Festival and has experience in performing, youth work, education and community theatre.

Nandita Ghose was brought up in Sussex and began writing plays and poems at school. She studied theatre at Dartington College where she wrote *The Company* and *Woman Who Foresaw her own Death* (for radio). *Ishtar Descends* was produced by the Albany Empire and directed by Sue Glanville. Nandita has just completed a new play, *Land*, and is presently a community theatre worker for Gemini Arts Company in West London.

Pauline Jacobs is twenty-seven and has lived and worked in Lewisham all her life. She co-wrote *Just Like Mohicans* with Trix Worrell, about the issues of racism and youth, which was performed at the Albany Empire in 1983 and produced by Channel 4. She began writing poetry and set up *The Blue Foot Writers Group*. *A Slice of Life* was scripted from improvisation around the theme of Black Self Image and was produced and performed by Second Wave at the Albany Empire in October 1985. It subsequently toured London and Amsterdam. Pauline now works as a young women's development worker.

Lisselle Kayla: 'Twenty-five years ago I made the journey to Kingston, Jamaica – a wide-eyed five year old. Through my writing I now trace the past years of a life I have shared with others fashioned by this unique corner in black migratory history. Infected by the sustained humour of all our parents, and affected by the origins of this humour in unfulfilled hopes and great sacrifice, I strive to acknowledge the value of these sturggles which we can only now appreciate.

'Now part of this chain, my daughter forms another

link. I hope that along with her own generation, my novel, journalistic, script and play-writing images will open her eyes to the wonder of the past flowing into the present. My thanks to all those who stood and are standing by me. But especially to Charlie, Pam, Paul, Val and my daughter Naomie.'

Cathy Kilcoyne founded Second Wave 1981–4, and co-scripted *A Netful of Holes* in 1984. With a background in mixed youth theatre, Cathy set up Second Wave to provide a platform for young women to explore freely and develop their own creative ideas. Second Wave produced three devised plays: *Spirit Level*, *Taking Five* and *A Netful of Holes*. *A Netful of Holes* – the most ambitious project – involved nine months research. First performed at the Albany Empire, Second Wave toured *A Netful of Holes* around hostels for homeless women, and have produced a video of scenes and discussions from the play (Albany Video).

Cathy has worked as a freelance writer, director and performer with Clean Break, The Sadista Sisters and Gay Sweatshop theatre companies. She is currently studying drama at Exeter University.

Angie Milan was brought up in East London, two miles from Leyton: 'The best bit about Leyton was the Youth Club, the skin-heads, reggae, 'bovver' and getting off with the boys. I had a mate, she was fourteen and going out with Orlando. I fancied him like mad and couldn't wait for him to drop her. After a couple of months she fell pregnant and he asked me out. I'd gone off him by then . . . I'll never forget how lucky I felt that it wasn't me.'

Carole Pluckrose set up Arc Theatre with her husband Clifford Oliver. Their intention was to promote new writing. Carole was pregnant throughout the tour of

Fallen and Grace was born in March 1987.

Fallen was written collaboratively. Polly Teale and Carole did the research together and spent three months experimenting with the material through improvisation in a workshop environment. Eventually Polly wrote the text using some of this work plus other sources.

Robyn Slovo is a playwright, editor and professional reader. She co-wrote *The Contract* for the Basement Youth Theatre produced by the Albany Empire in 1982. In 1984 she co-scripted *A Netful of Holes* and in 1986 became a member of the organising committee for the first Second Wave Festival of Young Women Playwrights.

Polly Teale grew up in Sheffield. She graduated from Manchester University Drama Department in 1985 after winning the Sunday Times Playwrighting Award for her play *Growing Pains*. Her second play, *Silent Night*, is published by Heinemann. Since *Fallen* she has written a screenplay, *Different for Girls*, and is presently Paines Plough The Writers Company's writer in residence.

Marie Elaine Wilson is twenty-one years old and was brought up in Sheffield. She studies at Rose Bruford Community Arts Theatre, toured theatre in schools and community centres in Yorkshire for three years with In The Bag Theatre Company, and acted in a Play for Today for BBC TV. She has written a play called *The Friendly Society* based on the lives of the Tolpuddle Martyrs for Sheffield Youth Theatre, and an adaptation for children of Shakespeare's *The Tempest*. Recently she was commissioned to write a new play called *Living it Up* for Touch and Go Theatre Company and is currently doing devised work with Sheffield Youth Theatre.